Even to a Jellyfish

by

James Sleckman

Cover Art by *The Wild Rose Press, Inc.*

The Wild Rose Press, Inc.
PO Box 708
Adams Basin, NY 14410-0708
Visit us at www.thewildrosepress.com

Publishing History
First Edition, 2024
Trade Paperback ISBN 978-1-5092-5601-3
Digital ISBN 978-1-5092-5602-0

Published in the United States of America

Dedication

To Cathy, my wife, my rock.

Acknowledgements

I am so grateful to my special friend, Anna. I couldn't have done this without you.

Thanks also to Randy, Mike and Tom, my fishing buddies.

Life is a beautiful, magnificent thing, even to a jellyfish....

The trouble is you won't fight. You've given up.

But there's something just as inevitable as death. And that's life.

Think of the power of the universe – turning the Earth, growing the trees.

That's the same power in you,

If you'll only have the courage and will to use it.

Charlie Chaplin

Chapter One

When we finally motored the boat to Steve's dock, it was well after midnight. A song by Green Day was in my head, something about the unpredictability of life. It had been a long day, and every one of my old bones kept reminding me that I was past my prime. Cops, guns and pot were not what I had expected for my first year of retirement.

All I really wanted to do was fish.

Chapter Two

"Bam! Fish on!"

"You got something already, Timbo?" asked Rob.

"You betcha," I said. "Tell Steve to put the engine in neutral so I can pull this sucker up.

"I hear you," came a voice from behind the wheel. "But it's probably a small striper. They're all over the place. I've been watching guys fly-fishing for them off the beach."

"I don't think so, Steve-O," I shouted. "This feels like a fluke. It's heavy and it hit me on the bottom."

"Holy shit!" yelled Rob. "Look at your rod; it's almost bent in half."

"Yeah, and I only have four-pound test on this reel; this rig's not meant to pull in a big fish. Get me the net."

Rob looked around. "Timbo, I gave you the net when we were in the garage. Where'd you put it?"

"Oh shit!" I said. "I think I left it there. When you came by, lugging that behemoth ice-chest from the 50s, I thought you were gonna have a heart attack, so I dropped the net to help you and forgot to go back for it. *Shit! Shit! Shit!*"

"Wow, look at the size of this monster. It's a regular doormat," I said, gloating. "Must be close to thirty inches. This one's definitely a keeper."

"Holy crap," screamed Steve. "How are you gonna

get this flatty on board? I just spent a hundred bucks for us to enter the Great Peconic Bay Tournament. We got a money-fish on the line, and because this idiot brings that stupid cooler from *Beach Blanket Bingo*, Timbo forgets the net."

Robert Riley's Irish skin turned red. About five years my senior, Rob was a gangly, retired New York City fireman who spent many hours on the water either fishing or clamming. "Hey. I was in charge of getting the bait."

"Shut up, you guys. This is serious. Where are my gloves? I'm gonna try to pull it in by hand."

"Never happen, Timbo," cracked Steve.

"You got a better idea?"

Steve stared at me with ugly eyes.

I turned to Rob. "Here, hold my pole. Keep the fish on top of the water. I'm gonna reach in and grab it by the gills."

"Yeah, right!" jeered Steve.

"You just shut up and steer," I yelled back.

"I'm trying, but the wind is pushing us straight to those boats over there," he said.

I stood on the swim platform and lowered myself into a crouch position. "Keep it steady. I almost got it. Just a little closer."

The boat lurched forward. I fell into the water and landed with a loud splash.

Rob hollered, "Shut off that engine."

Silence followed.

"Oh shit. Is that blood?"

For a moment, I had him in my hands, but suddenly my hooked fish and I were headed for the bowels of the sea. Instinct took over. I dove deep to get as far away as I could from the motor and prop. Boat propellers have bitten off more people's legs than sharks. The engine stopped; I surfaced about ten yards away and began swimming towards the stern. "Drop the ladder, Rob."

"You bleeding?"

I looked down at my leg. "Just my knee. Must've scraped it on the way in. Any sign of my fish?"

"Gone. The line snapped."

"Damn, that was a nice fluke. We gotta go back to the house and get the net. We don't stand a chance of winning the contest without it."

"Good, I think I left my sandwich in the car," Rob said.

"You forgot your sandwich? What the hell's in that cooler, anyway?" snickered Steve.

"Stuff. Important stuff!"

We headed back for the net and the sandwich. Melting on the dock was the bag of ice I had left behind.

"You guys forgot that, too?" Steve yelped, clearly exasperated.

"Screw you," Rob retorted with a laugh. "At least we didn't forget the beer."

We headed out again, this time for some serious fishing. Fluke, also known as summer flounder, is one of the tastiest fish in the waters off Long Island. When I started actively hooking them, some thirty years ago, they were so plentiful in our bays that every trip usually yielded a bucketful and a succulent dinner. No more. Rising water temperatures, climate change, and overfishing have made keeper fluke a rare commodity. Current regulations allow everyone three fish per day, each measuring nineteen inches head to tail. Last year we were lucky to hook one fish per trip.

We were expecting a crowd of boats at the Greenlawns, our favorite fishing grounds. It seemed many of the locals always caught a twenty-four-hour bug on opening day. Although fluke season lasted till mid-September, everyone knew that the first days were the best for grabbing a big one. We anchored off the west side of Shelter Island, where two huge houses with large lawns of green grass hugged the shoreline. Yeah, fishermen are not very creative when naming their spots.

We were three old salts enjoying a lazy day of retirement, me on the bow, Rob manning the stern, and Steve Lombardi at the wheel of his brand-new boat, *Kiss My Bass*. Mine was christened *Catey with a Sea*, after my better half, who enjoyed driving the boat more than I did. When we three amigos weren't pulling up fish, which was often, we were usually busting each other's chops. We talked sports, women, music, politics. Occasionally—no, rarely— one of us might reveal a secret, a fear, a regret. Once or twice I came close but stayed silent. Bottom line, the real glue was our mutual love of the water.

"Is this the maiden voyage?" I yelled to Steve as he pushed the throttle forward.

"No, the wife and I went for a spin Saturday. We cruised around the bay for about twenty minutes before Ginny felt cold."

"Wasn't it eighty degrees that day?"

"Yeah, and she had two sweatshirts on," he complained. "I didn't even get a chance to put my pole in the water."

"When was the last time you broke in a virgin boat?" I shouted to Rob.

He just smiled and nodded. He was either oblivious to our conversation or he wasn't wearing his hearing aids.

Surprisingly, the Greenlawns wasn't very crowded. Steve maneuvered his way between other boats until he found the right water depth and a sandy bottom before shutting down the engine. I took my position in the front, grabbing my rod and the net.

"Hey, where you going with that?" barked Steve.

"To show you losers how to catch some fish."

Steve is a few years older than me. He moved here about five years ago from Philadelphia, where he was a big wig in the snack industry, pretzels, especially chocolate covered ones, being his specialty. He retired out east to enjoy the peace and solitude of the North Fork. One Saturday morning, a few years back, my wife Catey came home from spin class and informed me that we were going out to dinner with a couple named Ginny and Steve.

"Who?" I replied.

"Don't worry; you'll like them."

Conversation over.

So on a blustery November evening, with the Jets clinging to a three-point lead over the Bills, I grudgingly left my armchair and drove to Greenport. At Claudio's, the girls made the introductions, and we sat at a window table. I could tell that Steve was also grumpy, but a pint of red ale and some football talk soon erased the scowl on his face. Steve is a big time Giants fan so his mission that night was to get home before their eight o'clock game. It turned out to be a pleasant evening, and, on the way home, Catey flashed me the same smile I fell in love with forty years ago. The Jets lost that night, but what else is new? I was hoping to score!

"Bang! I just got a hit," I yelled. "Fish on!"

My right hand started to work the reel.

"You need the net?" asked Rob, looking around. "Where the hell did I put it?"

"Why don't you look in your cooler?" mumbled Steve, and we all lost it.

For the next few minutes, Steve and I kept pulling up shorts.

"I can't believe I haven't had a single bite," moaned Rob, reeling up his rig and empty hook. Grabbing a strip of squid, he turned to us and confessed, "You know, I was so frigging excited about opening day that I think I forgot to bait my hook before."

"Yeah, I can't remember shit anymore," sighed Steve, his tone suddenly sympathetic. "I went to the hardware store the other day and forgot why I was there. I walked around the aisles for fifteen minutes, feeling totally frustrated. I finally picked up some garbage bags and left. When I got home, I couldn't open the garage door. The remote needed batteries."

"Well, I still can't believe I forgot the fishing net!" I said. "I never forgot stuff like that."

"Welcome to my world," said Steve. "I used to pride myself on remembering the names of all my customers and all the sales reps. Now, I can hardly remember the names of my grandkids."

"Yeah, but I forgot the frigging net!" I yelped. "We could have won the whole shebang. Got our pictures on the cover of *The Long Island Fisherman* and become heroes to all the old guys out there. Now some millennial with perfect teeth and an eight-hundred-dollar rod and reel will be explaining how he used his fish-finding app to land his trophy using a wad of gulp."

"Don't worry about it, Timbo," said Rob. "I have the same problem and it seems to be getting worse each day. Sometimes, I hear a song on the radio and I can't remember a thing. When it came to music, I used to know every band, every vocalist and every song. Not anymore. This getting old stuff really sucks."

I started reeling up another fish.

"You need the net?" he asked. We all burst out laughing again.

"Nah. It feels light," I said, bringing it in anyway.

"It's just a jellyfish," said Rob.

"Just a jellyfish? Hey, this could be the answer to our problems," I said.

"What are you talking about?" asked Rob.

I continued, "Haven't you seen that TV commercial about a drug that's supposed to curb memory loss? I see it all the time when I watch the news. They say that it's made from jellyfish."

"Yeah, I've seen it too," said Steve, "but I can't remember the name of the drug. I think it begins with a P."

"Now that's funny," chuckled Rob. "A drug that improves your memory that we can't remember the name of? You can't make this shit up."

****

We spent the next few hours floating around the bay picking up an assortment of fish, most of them throwbacks. Rob latched on to a keeper about twenty inches in size, big enough for dinner but too small to enter the contest. When it started to drizzle, we called it a day, motored up to the dock and began cleaning the boat and filleting the fish.

Steve blurted out, "Pearlagen!"

"Yeah. Sue and I saw them at the Garden back in '98."

"No you jackass, that's the name of that drug. Next time wear you hearing aids."

****

That night I couldn't sleep. I tossed and turned and thought about the day. I still couldn't believe that I had forgotten that damn net. That was a nice fish. Things like that seem to be happening to me more often these days. Stupid stuff, like forgetting my socks when I go to play golf or leaving the basement lights on all night. Rob is right. This getting old stuff really sucks. I propped myself up on my pillow and looked at the moonlight reflected on the water. I smiled to myself and thought of so many midnight swims with Catey and our son Kev; of full moon kayak rides with friends; of glorious sunrises over Bug Light; of predawn fishing trips to Plum Gut. Yeah, aging sucks, but it beats the alternative. I glanced at my Catey sleeping soundly and thought, "Who's got it better than me?"

****

The next morning, I took my kayak and paddled out to the channel. The water glistened. Occasionally, a stray fish, probably a small striper or a blue, broke the surface. I made my way towards Mud Island, inhabited solely by a pair of ospreys who have lived and fished here for many years. As I drifted closer, the female screeched trying to ward off my approach, while her mate hovered in the air hunting for breakfast. I kept my distance. I turned left into a narrow canal where the water was very still. This was a feasting spot for mosquitos during July and August, but today it was perfect. Farther down the channel, I noticed the surface was becoming cloudy. Had summer algae arrived early? Were crabs disturbing the sandy bottom? I stopped and dipped my paddle a few feet under. At first, I noticed nothing unusual, but then I spotted a school of moon jellyfish. Interesting.

They were small, milky white, almost translucent, ranging in size from a silver dollar to a soup can lid. I scooped one out of the water and put it in the palm of my hand. Surprisingly, there were no stingers; so I filled my container to the brim and headed home.

When I got back, I sat on the dock, started humming an old Otis Redding tune and took a jelly out for a closer look. It was neither slimy nor slippery. When I patted its sides with my tee shirt, it dried out quickly. There were tiny pores on top, and the bottom was rough with crevices. Around the rim were a bunch of openings, probably necessary for survival. I tossed the creature from one hand to the other and thought, "What the heck?" I took a deep breath, closed my eyes, and opened my mouth. With one big gulp, I swallowed the whole thing.

Chapter Three

It tasted salty. As it navigated past my tonsils, the jellyfish squiggled down my gullet and plopped into my stomach. It was different from a raw clam or an oyster, not mushy but soft and firm like a slice of banana. I felt the coarse backside of the fish hug the edge of my windpipe. Next time, I thought, I should cut it in half.

Next time? What the hell am I thinking? I just ate a raw jellyfish. Is this thing poisonous? Should I chug some water? Stick my finger down my throat?

As the minutes passed, I calmed down and started smiling. I pounded my chest and yelled out to no one, "*Fear Factor*, here I come." I flashed back to my keg party days in college when I swallowed a live goldfish. That next morning, I was sick as a dog, but, then again, it could have been the shots of tequila.

I moseyed over to the outdoor shower and let hot water soothe my old bones. Still grinning, and with a towel around my waist, I walked into the kitchen. There was Catey in her standard retirement uniform, a beat-up Block Island sweatshirt and cut-offs. "What's so funny?" she asked, a smile in her sapphire eyes.

"Nothing," I said, moving closer and squeezing her tight. "It's just that I'm feeling manly."

"Sure doesn't feel that way," she teased, pulling me toward her to whisper in my ear."What were you doing down there," she asked, ruining my Tarzan moment.

"Uh, nothing," I stammered.

"Nothing? You were down there for a really long time."

"The killies are finally here, so I rigged up my trap. Now I'll have live bait—a gourmet dinner if you're a flatfish."

"Speaking of dinner, are you fishing with the guys today?"

"No, things are pretty slow out there. The water's still too cold. But I may do some clamming this afternoon when the tide goes out."

"Linguini with clam sauce tonight?"

"Great minds think alike," I said and winked.

****

Up until last year, before I retired from my job as a sales rep, I had time for only a quick morning jog twice a week. Now, at sixty-seven, I exercise first thing every day. I kayak, bike, swim or paddle board. And, for the last two weeks, I've had a jellyfish for breakfast. This morning, just before my first bite, I heard, "What's up, buddy?"

"Holy shit! You scared me."

There was Martin Edwards, my next-door neighbor. This was Marty's first full season on the North Fork. He retired from the courts at the end of December, sold his pricey apartment in the city, and moved into his summer home full-time. He was thin, average height, with traces of a new beard. Sporting gold-rimmed John Lennon glasses, Marty was the only guy my age without gray hair. He was bald on top with a wispy man bun.

"You trying to give me a heart attack?"

"I didn't mean to sneak up on you."

"What the hell you doing out here this early?" I said, quickly hiding my Swiss army knife.

"Just going for my daily swim."

"I'm thinking about taking the boat out later today. People are starting to catch some big fish over by the ferry dock. Wanna join me?"

"Love to."

I started to leave.

"Hold on a sec," Marty said. "Can I ask you something?"

I turned around.

"I've been watching you. You got some weird ritual going on out here?"

I looked at him curiously. "You got nothing better to do than spy on me?"

"I'm not spying on you. I'm checking with my binoculars to see if the Goddamned purple martins have moved into that thousand-dollar birdhouse the wife bought. Pam has become obsessed with her orioles and finches. Between the effing felted feeders, her squirrel-proof poles and hanging hummingbird houses, I can't even see my boat anymore."

I smiled. "In that case, can you keep a secret?"

"You know I can't, but I'll give it a shot."

"I've been eating these," I said, pulling up my fish cage.

"Jellyfish? What the hell? You trying to increase your sperm count or something?"

"No. It's for my memory."

"Memory? You're kidding me, right?"

"Well, I have been remembering better. Last night Catey and I were watching *Jeopardy*, and I was on fire.

I got all the tough questions, and fast."

"Yeah, like what?"

"Like 'Who played Trixie on the *Honeymooners*?' and 'Who was the only president with English as a second language?'"

"So wait, let me get this straight. Out of the blue, you just decided to start wolfing down jellyfish from the creek?"

"Well, sort of. I was seeing all these TV commercials about this drug derived from jellyfish that improves your memory. So I decided to try them."

"Raw? You are certifiably insane."

"Probably."

"So what do they taste like?"

"Not bad, like a salty oyster."

"And do they really improve your memory?"

"Try me. Think of a song that you liked growing up. Sing me a few lines and I'll name the artist."

He thought for a minute, then started singing about a guy walking in the rain.

"That's too easy. Del Shannon. I would have known that last month."

"All right, how about this one?

Marty started snapping his fingers. Soon as he opened his mouth, I realized he couldn't carry a tune for nothing. "When this old—"

"Stop," I yelled, covering my ears. "The Drifters."

"Shit!"

"Try again."

"Here's one you'll never remember." Marty crouched down and spread his arms wide and began serenading me with a song about a famous Brooklyn amusement park.

"The Excellents," I answered quickly. "Unless you mean the Lou Reed redo from the seventies."

"I can't believe you knew that. How?"

"I told you, my man, my memory's gotten so much better. It's like I'm thirty-five again."

"Hm. Did you have one yet?"

"Not y-e-t," I sang, smirking.

"Okay, I'll be right back."

Marty returned with a tall glass of bubbly.

"Champagne?"

"No, seltzer, but mostly vodka. I figured the alcohol would kill that sucker as soon as it hits my belly."

I carefully removed a live jelly from the bucket, sliced it in half, and handed it to him. He took a sip of his liquid courage and slurped the creature down his throat, coughing once. I swallowed what was left, savoring the briny flavor. I had started to acquire a taste for these suckers.

"You look like you enjoyed that."

"Grows on you," I said, smacking my lips.

"So, fishing this afternoon?"

"Yep, I'll text you when I'm ready to head out."

He started walking back to his house, but after a few steps, he stopped and turned. "Hey, Timbo, which president learned English as a second language?"

"Martin Van Buren."

"Shit! I should have known that!"

"You're right, M-A-R-T-I-N."

I sat there at the end of the dock, my feet dangling in the water. Memory, like everything else, I thought, can be a double-edged sword.

Chapter Four

It was the summer of 1980. Out of college for six years, still single, I was living with my buddies in a beach house on the Great South Bay. I had finally found my calling as a manufacturer's rep in the electronics industry and was making decent money. Wire, electrical connectors, and cable ties were my specialty. Traveling the northeast in my company car, a new four-door sedan, I thought I was King Shit.

Two years earlier, on the Sunday afternoon of Memorial Day weekend, I had, literately, fallen into a blonde at the Boardy Barn happy hour. We started talking, realized that we had friends in common, and began seeing each other. Tonight, I was planning on popping the question at the site of our first dinner date. It was going to be a surprise, and I was more nervous about the size of the ring than about what her answer was going to be.

I was finishing up my Saturday chores, when the house phone rang.

"Hello."

"Hey, Timbo. It's Vinny. I'm in trouble!"

Vinny also known as Crazy Vinny, was one of my oldest friends. He owned a tree service, worked hard all week, and partied harder all weekend.

"You're in trouble?"

"Yeah. My boat died. Ran out of gas."

"Where are you?"

"Flower Beach. I need a tow.

"Yeah, but, Vinny. I've got plans."

"Only take an hour, tops. I really need your help. Please."

Shit. This had to happen today? I calculated how long this would take and figured if I left right away, I'd have enough time.

"Okay. I'll be right there."

"Thanks, Timbo. You're a lifesaver."

The water was flat as I maneuvered the seventeen-foot whaler out back off the dock. I had been to Flower Beach many times and I knew it was a straight shot in open water. Passing by the Scallop Grounds, I honked hello to a couple of teenagers using their feet to dig clams.

I made my way around the bend, and there was Vinny, nursing a shiner. "What the hell happened?"

"Long story. Remember Cindy?"

"Backseat Cindy?"

"Yeah. I was with her last night."

"Isn't she married? To Fisticuffs Foley?"

"Yeah. And it ain't pretty."

After I tied a rope from Vinny's bow to my stern and got him to the ramp without a hitch, Vinny jumped off. "I owe you one."

"Just tell me, was the black eye worth it?"

"She still loves me." He grinned.

I checked my watch. It was a little after eleven when I passed Flower Beach again, now crowded with sunbathers. The clammers were still out there. One of them was waving his arms excitedly. I gave them a thumb's up and headed home.

That evening, at a corner table at The Seafood Barge, with a Roberta Flack classic playing in the background, I got down on one knee. Before I could finish asking, Catey said, "Yes." And the ring was perfect. We spent a romantic evening planning our future. In the morning, while she was still asleep, I stepped out to get us coffee. The headlines of Sunday's paper read, *Young Man Drowns Clamming in Bay*.

I read further. An eyewitness had reported that the two teens were clamming by Flower Beach, when suddenly the sandy bottom turned into muck. Neither of the brothers could swim, but one managed to make it to solid ground. He later told police that he had tried to flag down passing speed boaters, but nobody stopped. Suddenly, I felt sick to my stomach.

Chapter Five

On the days I wasn't fishing or cruising the bays, I was usually at the Links. I'd been playing golf for the past forty years but didn't get serious about the game till I retired. Recently, I've been introducing the finer points of the sport to my fishing buddies.

A few mornings after my breakfast with Marty, Steve and I decided to play a quick nine holes. He had just taken his first lesson of the season and was anxious to test his new skills.

"So how did your lesson go?"

"Great, Timbo. I found out that my set-up was all out of whack. The pro adjusted my stance, and all of a sudden, everything started to fall into place."

"That's terrific."

I smacked my drive down the center of the fairway. "You're up."

Steve popped a chocolate bonbon in his mouth and placed his new ball on the tee. He stood over the target and took a practice swing. Staring long and hard at the ball, he muttered, "Shit. I can't remember a thing the pro told me. Do I put my hands here or there? And what about my feet? I'm so lost."

"Just relax. Take an easy swing and it'll all come back to you."

Steve raised his club and struck the ball, solid and with authority. It went high in the air and plopped into the pond on the right. He hit another, and the ball faded again, this time landing in the tall grass.

"Not bad," I said, as we strolled down the fairway for our second shots.

A look of frustration crossed his face. "Yeah, but you should have seen me yesterday at the driving range. Every shot was going straight and a hell of a lot farther. Today, I'm all over the frigging place."

Steve was the most relaxed of my Southold friends. Almost six feet, he still had an athletic build but had gained a few pounds since his surfing days. His large mop of salt and pepper hair and his Fu Manchu mustache made him look like an old Joe Namath.

"Calm down, buddy. It's just golf. We all have our bad days."

"Hey, remember the other day, on the boat, when we were talking about that memory drug? I looked into it."

I looked at him quizzically, "You did?"

"Yeah. I'm desperate. I can't remember anything and it's driving me nuts."

"And what did you learn?"

"First thing, it ain't covered by Medicare or my secondary insurance. It cost like fifty bucks a pill. That's like three grand for a two-month's supply. Do you believe that shit?"

"You know, I think I've found something else that works."

"Really?"

"Maybe," I said, smiling. "Remember that school of white jellyfish we saw in the bay?"

"You mean those moon jellies?"

"Yeah."

"What about them?"

"Turned my head to make sure no one was approaching. I leaned in and whispered, "I've been eating them.""

"You what?"

"Every morning."

"You trying to grow a third ball or something?"

"I don't think so," I said, staring at my crotch.

"How long have you been doing this?"

"Couple weeks, maybe more."

"And it's working?"

"I think so. I can remember all sorts of stuff from my past, and I'm kicking ass on *Jeopardy*. I've even turned Marty on to them."

"Marty's eating them, too? You're kidding me."

"No, really."

"I can't believe a smart guy like him would do a stupid thing like that. You, I can believe. And is it working for him?"

"I don't know. He only started a few days ago. Washes it down with a glass of vodka."

"Marty washes everything down with a glass of vodka. What do they taste like?"

"Kinda like raw clams or salty oysters."

"Really?"

"Yeah, I've always liked salty things. I grew up in a house with five brothers and sisters and I was always hungry. When my mother got home from the grocery store on Saturdays, anything sweet or salty was history. A box of cookies—gone soon as it was opened. Chips and pretzels—never had a chance. Occasionally, a can of mixed nuts would last till Sunday, and we always ate them in the same order. Cashews first. Then peanuts.

Then the almonds and the filberts, those round ones about the size of a marble. Last to go were the Brazil nuts, the big ones that looked and tasted like garden stones but were edible because they were salty."

"Timbo, what's this got to do with jellyfish?"

"Just bear with me. At the end of my street was the main road, Park Avenue. It had streetlights and traffic, and my mom warned me never to cross it alone, but the gas station on the other side had a machine that sold nuts. It was an old gumball machine; you put a nickel in the slot, turned the crank and out popped a handful of nuts. I saw kids using it whenever my dad filled up."

"Where the hell you going with this?"

"You'll see. One day, when I was about six, I had a craving for something salty. It was summertime, my brothers were gone, and my mom was doing something girly with my sisters. I searched all the kitchen cabinets for something to eat but struck out. Not even a measly saltine. I went upstairs, stole a couple of nickels from my brother's coin collection, and ran down the street to the gas station. At the nut machine, I slowly put my nickel into the slot, on the cashew side, turned the crank all the way to the right, and, out of the chute, five little nuts trickled into the palm of my hand."

"You're killing me, Timbo."

But there was no stopping me. "As I was glaring at my open hand, the man who owned the place walked by. 'The price of cashews has really gone up, son; try the other side; you'll do better.' At six years old, I was not a very adventurous eater, but five nuts wasn't gonna cut it. The other side had pistachios. So I put in my second nickel and turned the crank. Bingo! I heard them flow down the chute, and as I opened the flap, I got a huge handful of red nuts. There were so many, I couldn't fit them in my palm so the extras I stuffed in my pocket. I pulled out the first one, still in its shell, cracked it open with my fingernails, and placed it in my mouth. Wow! I can still remember that salty taste of my first pistachio nut. It still brings a smile to my face. Then I ran across the street, settled down on a log under a shady tree and polished off what was left in my pockets. When I finished, I moseyed my way back home for a cool drink of water."

"Does this story ever end?"

"Soon. Soon. Have another chocolate."

I kept talking. "So I go home, walk into my kitchen, and my mom gives me the once over. I knew something was wrong. She started pounding me with questions, asking where I had been all day and why my lips and shirt were so red. I kept silent, but I looked down and noticed that my white tee shirt looked bloodstained, and my fingernails were dark pink. I was getting kinda nervous. Then she stared at me and wanted to know what I had been eating. When I said 'pistachios,' she went nuts."

Steve didn't laugh.

"Nuts, get it?"

Steve still didn't laugh.

"Then she asked where I got them and when I told her from the gas station on the main road, she got really pissed. She couldn't believe that I had crossed that busy street without getting hit by a car. I really didn't want to tell her, but I was caught red-handed."

I looked at Steve, waiting for a smile or something. Instead he said, "You got a razor in that golf bag? I want to slit my wrists."

"Almost done Steve-O. Then she told me to put my shirt in the hamper, wash my hands, and go to my room and wait until my father got home. It took a while to get the red stuff off. I had to scrub real hard. When my dad came home that night, he lectured me about the danger of crossing the street, but I could tell his heart wasn't really in it. My older brothers thought it was pretty stupid, but, actually, pretty cool."

"That's it? And what about the jellyfish?"

"They're salty!"

"That's fucking it?"

I started laughing, as Steve scoffed down another sweet. He shook his head in disbelief.

I picked up his discarded wrapper. "You really like these, don't you?"

"Better than some of the food Ginny's been serving me. She's trying to get me on this plant-based diet. The other day she made me a pizza and covered it with white beans. Tasted like cardboard. An hour later I wolfed down two bowls of ice cream, behind her back, of course. I don't know whether she's trying to starve me or poison me. You say these jellyfish are really helping you remember things?"

"Yeah, seems like they're working for me."

"Got any extras?"

"Sure, after that story, you deserve one. We'll hit my dock on the way home. I haven't had my morning fix yet."

"They're salty. That's the dumbest thing I ever heard."

As Steve pulled into my driveway, I saw Marty heading to the dock, morning cocktail in hand.

"Hey guys. How was golf today?"

"The weather was perfect, but my game sucked. Hey, Timbo tells me you've been gulping jellyfish?"

"Yeah, I figured it was worth a shot."

"Is it working?"

"Don't know yet! I just started a few days ago."

"No side effects?"

"Besides making me horny? No."

"Okay, Timbo, give me two. And maybe a shot of vodka."

I laughed.

"Joining the club, are you?" asked Marty.

"Timbo says they're helping him remember all kinds of things, and God knows I can't remember shit anymore."

"Yeah, he's turning into Mister Memory."

I took the jellies out of my trap. "Ready Steve-O?"

"Ready as I'll ever be."

"Wanna eat it whole, or should I slice it in half?"

"Got a tiny one?"

I handed him one the size of a silver dollar. "How's this?"

"Fine. I guess," he said, studying the slimy creature he was about to ingest.

"Hold on a sec," cried Marty. "On the count of three. One, two, three."

"Mm, mm good," he said. "And now, I'm going in to attack my wife."

I turned to Steve. "So what d'ya think?"

"I can't believe I ate the whole thing. Saltier, chewier than I expected, but I've tasted worse. If you could spare a couple, I'll put them in my morning smoothie, drown out the taste of that kale and quinoa."

I tossed a few into a plastic bag.

"Fishing tomorrow, Timbo?"

"Sounds good."

"Let's take my boat. I'll ask Rob and Marty. Sure would be nice to catch a few fluke."

"Fluke. That reminds me of a day…."

Steve ran!

Chapter Six

The following morning the four anglers cruised out of Steve's canal in search of keeper fluke. The weather was gray and overcast but unusually warm for the end of May. We knew that we were in for a good fishing day when Marty and Rob each picked up a keeper on the first drift. Rob's was a beast, measuring over twenty-five inches. Our next drift was quick, resulting in three fish, all a tad too short. On our third try, we headed north, giving us a longer swing across the grounds. Out of the corner of my eye, I spied a small boat run aground on the beach.

Before I even pointed this out, Marty said, "That looks like Socket's skiff."

Socket—nobody called him by his real name—was a "local" who worked as a bay-man all summer and did odd jobs during the winter to stay afloat. He was tall, almost six-two, and weighed about one-fifty soaking wet. With his thin head of white hair and bulging, brown eyes, he looked almost ghostly. And always, he wore a faded green army jacket. He owned a small cottage by Hog's Neck and loved to tool around in his eighteen-foot clam boat.

When Socket wasn't fishing, he was drunk, or stoned, or both. Rumor has it, he was watching TV with his buddies on December 1, 1969 when his birthdate, July 19, hit number one in the Vietnam lottery. Socket stayed up all that night, got really shift-faced, and hatched a plan to join the Navy. The next morning, he drove thirty miles to the local recruitment office and camped out till the doors opened. In not so fine form, he shuffled in and signed the enlistment papers. On his way out the door, the officer in charge hollered, "Sober up, son; you're in the Army now."

Dazed and confused, Socket looked up and saw the Navy office was next door.

"I guess his father wasn't a senator," sneered Marty.

"Yeah. CCR nailed it with that tune," chimed Rob.

Socket's experience in Vietnam was a mystery. Some said he took a bullet to his leg, hence the slight limp, but no one knows for sure. He spends his afternoons in the VFW hall drinking bottles of beer and his evenings on his front porch sipping whiskey. And, he always has weed. Really good weed to forget.

"Something doesn't seem right," said Marty. "Looks like he's stuck on that sandbar. Let's check it out."

Steve steered towards the bar and carefully pulled up alongside. "Shit! Look at all this blood."

Collapsed on the deck was Socket, bleeding profusely from a large gash on the side of his forehead. He was unconscious. I took off my shirt and applied pressure to the wound. "Steve, call 911!"

Minutes later, Steve got off the horn and yelled, "They told me not to move him. Just drive his boat over to Port Marina. EMTs from the local fire department will meet us at the dock."

Rob jumped into the shallows and pushed us off the bar. Marty took the wheel, gliding Socket's boat around to the rendezvous point with Steve following close behind. Once tied up, we were met by the medical responders, who placed Socket on a gurney and stuffed him into the ambulance. I tied the small boat to an empty piling while Marty talked to the lead paramedic. After the ambulance took off to the nearest ER, we headed back out on the water.

"What do you think happened to him?" asked Rob.

"They think that it may have been a stroke," offered Marty. "Apparently, he collapsed on the deck and hit his head on the side of the console."

Steve looked concerned. "That gash was really nasty. You think he'll be okay?"

"It doesn't look good," sighed Marty.

"Hey Timbo, what was Socket's real name, anyway?" asked Rob.

"John Toomey."

"That Irish?"

"I think so."

"How the hell did he get the nickname Socket? Was he an electrician?"

"Funny, but no."

"Was he a mechanic?"

"A mechanic?"

"Yeah, like a socket wrench?"

"No, you jackass. Lots of kids were called John back then, so they all had nicknames."

"I still don't get it," said Rob, looking totally confused.

The aging hippie, Rob, was a bit of a space cadet. Dressed in his typical cargo pants, he always wore a tee shirt that he got from some concert. Today, he sported an Allman Brothers number—black, red and frayed at the collar.

"You been smoking that wacky weed today? Think of Socket as his first name."

Rob started thinking out loud, "Socket Toomey, Socket Toomey, Socket Toomey." All of a sudden, he gave out a gut-busting laugh. "Now I get it—sock it to me—from that old time TV show. The one with that hot girl with the British accent. She was always saying that."

Raising an imaginary envelope to my forehead, a-la Carnac the Magnificent, I said, "Judy Carne?"

"Yeah, and that other one. What was her name?"

"Goldie Hawn," I blurted.

"My God, Timbo. How do you remember these things?"

"Rob, it was Rowen and Martin's *Laugh In*. I immediately started rattling off the other stars: Artie Johnson, Ruth Buzzi, Lilly Tomlin, Henry Gibson and Joanne Worley. Oh and the announcer guy was Gary Owens."

When Rob just gaped at me, Marty said, "Maybe we should let him in on our secret."

"Might as well," said Steve. "He'll probably find out anyway."

"I've been eating moonies," I confessed. "To improve my memory."

"Moonies?"

"Jellyfish."

"You're shitting me."

"Marty and Steve, too."

"You're all nuts!" he said, twirling his finger by his ear. "Is it working?"

"Not yet, but I only started a few days ago," said

Steve.

"How about you, Marty?"

"Something is definitely happening to me."

"Yeah, he's getting horny and driving his wife crazy," snickered Steve.

"Maybe I should try them. My memory sucks and I haven't been horny in ….Well, let's just leave it at that."

"I gotta warn you though, they're kinda gross."

"That doesn't bother me. Back in the sixties, I put so much foreign shit into my body that I'm surprised I'm still alive. Pot, speed, hash, LSD, TCP and a hundred different kinds of mushrooms. And that's just for starters. Plus, before I discovered bourbon, I drank every kind of alcohol I could get my hands on."

Steve hung off the front of the boat, giving all of us a view of his plumber's crack. "I see a few moonies floating by. Get me the net."

When I grabbed the net from under the seat and handed it over, Rob looked at me with relief.

"Here you go," Steve handed Rob the gooey, translucent disk.

Rob placed the critter in the palm of his hand. "You really eat these things?"

"Yep," we all replied at once.

"Well, here goes nothing." He bit it in half.

"You don't eat it like a steak, jackass," said Steve. "Swallow it whole."

"Wrong! You must savor the exquisite flavors and spices of this unique experience," Rob expounded, theatrically, placing the remaining half in his mouth as if it was a Communion wafer. Former altar boy, that one.

"Not bad, but a little salty."

Steve glared at me, "Don't you dare tell that nut story again or I'll fucking kill you."

The tide slowed to a stop so we decided to pack it in. Once back on land, Marty was setting off to the hospital to check on Socket.

"I'm running low on jellies," I announced. "Anyone want to kayak later to search for more?"

"Sure."

"High tide is at seven. That work for everyone?"

"Perfect," said Marty. "The girls have book club tonight. I'll grab us a pizza and be at your place at six."

"I'll bring the beer," said Rob.

"Can we make it two pizzas?" pleaded Steve. "Ginny's making asparagus tacos for lunch."

Chapter Seven

At six that evening, Rob, Steve and I were popping open our first beers when Marty sauntered over. He was just back from the hospital and looking glum.

"How's Socket doing?" I asked.

"Not good," Marty mumbled. "His heartbeat is down to nothing and the doctors aren't sure if he'll make it through the night."

"Did he recognize you?"

"I don't think so. He kept calling me 'old man.'"

"But that's what you are, old man. That's what we all are. O-L-D."

"This whole thing sucks," Steve muttered. "The army thing did Socket in. He left college to play semi-pro ball, then got thrown in the draft pool, ends up in 'Nam and messes up his leg."

"Yeah, wrong place, wrong time," said Marty. "He coulda been on a baseball card. That's how good he was."

But sometimes, I thought to myself, it's being in the right place but at the wrong time, my past coming up to haunt me once again.

Rob interrupted my thoughts. "There was nothing good about that war. Young men, soldiers and flowers. Pete Seeger said it best."

We wolfed down the first pie and most of the second before starting our jellyfish hunt. The creek flattened out, the wind died, and patches of blue were peeking through the clouds. Luckily, there was a hint of a cool breeze, just enough to keep the no-see-ums from biting.

"Gonna be a beautiful night," said Marty, passing each of us a beer for the ride. He also handed us butterfly nets with matching pails stolen from his grandkids' closet. Mine was pink.

We headed out with me leading the way to the canal where I first found the jellies. Hoping to land a small bass or bluefish along the way, Marty and I had fishing poles attached to the back of our kayaks.

We were a sight to behold. I was wearing dark brown trunks, a chain store special, and Steve had on his too-tight, six-pocket cargo shorts stuffed with sweets. Marty was making a fashion statement clad in his expensive floral bathing suit. Rob was in the same clothes he wore fishing that morning.

"Aren't you hot in those long pants?" asked Steve.

"I'm very comfortable. These are lightweight, and, if you must know, I'm wearing my Lakeside Trading Company underwear."

"Those are the best drawers that I've ever owned! It's like going commando. Catey got them for me at Christmas."

"I never heard of them," said Steve.

"Oh, they're really comfortable," agreed Marty. "They're made out of organic cotton and have just a touch of spandex. Once you try them, you're hooked for life."

I felt a tug on my pole and started reeling in a small striper, but he spit the hook and took off. And, anyway, he was too small.

"I don't see anything," said Rob as we neared our destination.

"They were all over this place a few weeks ago."

"I see nothing," echoed Marty.

"Nada, Timbo" said Steve, dragging his net and coming up empty.

"Hold it, Steve," I said. "Try putting the net down deep; they might be in cooler water."

Looking skeptical, he did. "Holy shit! You're right," he yelled, "I got about ten of those suckers."

In no time, our buckets were overflowing with moonies.

"It looks like we got enough for a month," said Marty. "A real bonanza!"

"Now that was a great TV show," said Rob. "Every Sunday night at nine. I never missed it."

"Did you guys know that one of the stars of that show retired to the North Fork? Catey and I bumped into him at the farm stand a few times. True story, I swear."

"Hey Memory Man," called Rob. "What were the names of Ben's three sons?"

"That's easy—Adam, Hoss and Little Joe."

"Yeah, but the whole premise of that show was sort of strange, especially for the sixties," said Marty. "Three different sons from three different wives?"

"Three wives," mused Steve. "Who would want that? I'm one and done."

"Amen to that," I said.

"Hey, Baby Huey," yelled Steve. "Are those fancy underpants of yours boxers or briefs?"

"Boxers," replied Rob, trying to stand up to pull down his pants.

We were all cracking up when we heard a phone ring.

Marty answered, talked to someone, and announced, "Socket is gone."

Chapter Eight

The night returned to its silent state.

On our trek back to shore, I started singing that Harry Chapin ballad about a cab driver and, immediately, my three buddies joined in.

Harry, who coincidentally was from Long Island, recorded this tune in the late sixties. The song tells a story of a struggling hack, a contented working stiff who runs into a former lover, wealthy but unhappy. But it's also about hope and dreams and sex. It's a guy's song. The four of us finished out all the verses without missing a beat.

We returned the kayaks to my beach and gathered around the fire pit. I was about to pop open a brew when Marty cried out, "Put that beer away. This calls for the brown stuff." He ran into his house and came back with four plastic cups and a large bottle of top-shelf, dark rum.

My Catey had stumbled upon these spirits on a cruise about ten years earlier, and ever since it's been our go-to drink for warm summer nights. When mixed with the soda of choice, it's the perfect cocktail. That evening, we drank it neat and raised our glasses, "To Socket."

"I wonder how different my life would have been if I had been shipped out to 'Nam," I said.

"What was your lottery number?" asked Marty.

"Two-fifty-nine, but I wasn't in the first lottery. Remember, I'm a few years younger than you guys. By 1972 the war was already winding down. Chances of getting called if your number was over twenty were slim to none. It was just a formality at that point."

"I have a good story," piped up Steve. "I had just started my second semester of sophomore year at Rutgers. It sucked. I was living at home, commuting, and I was sick of frigging school. All I wanted to do was surf. When the chance came to be a beach bum on the West coast, I jumped on it."

"Who wouldn't?" nodded Rob.

"That spring and summer were great," Steve continued. "I lived in a house by the shore with a bunch of guys, worked part time for food and rent, and rode waves every day. When I got my grades in May, I was pleasantly surprised. I had passed! One course. With a C. I wasn't invited back, but I didn't give a damn. I was in California, riding four-foot swells everyday, and living the dream. Of course, all good things must come to an end."

"I know where this is going," said Marty.

"So that Thanksgiving, I showed up like a lost puppy on my parents' doorstep. When they asked about school or job prospects, I told them that I had everything under control. And then went to the bar. Truth was, I was a fucking wreck. And then, when I pulled a low number in the lottery, I was done for."

"How low?" I asked.

"Low enough that I knew I would have to go back to school. Rutgers wouldn't reinstate me. Said I would have to go to Mercer CC. Which I did. Only to find out that registration was closed. Fucking catch 22. Then they told me, go talk to your advisor. I didn't even know I had an advisor. But turns out I did, some guy dressed in a corduroy sports coat with patches on the elbows. You know the type."

"Oh yeah," I chuckled. "The wannabe cool professors that all the hot chicks suck up to for their A's."

"You got it. So he says to me, very seriously, 'Steve, last semester you stopped attending class in early March. You failed two subjects, got two incompletes, and one C, in Music Appreciation.'"

'Yes sir.'

'And you are an Economics major?'

'Yes sir.'

'And why did you drop out, son?'

'I moved to the West coast, sir.'

'Because?'

'I had an opportunity, sir.'

'To?'

'Surf in California, sir.'

"He leaned back in his chair and stared at me. 'And now you want to be reinstated?' he asked."

"'Yes sir,' I said, starting to sound like a broken record."

'Well, son, the only way to matriculate is to earn twelve credits, A's and B's only, and reapply next year.' There was a look on his face that reminded me of a poker player holding all the high cards."

'I tried that, sir. Registration is already closed.'

'It's out of my hands, young man.'

"I felt like punching this asshole. Instead, I played the pity card. 'Sir, you are my last hope. If I don't return to school this term, I'll be drafted and sent to

Vietnam, sir.'"

'What is your lottery number, son?'

"'Thirty-nine, sir.' Now I was begging. 'Sir, I know that I screwed up, but I did really well last year. Just let me back in. Please, I promise I'll graduate in three years.'"

"'It's not that easy,' he said, leaning back again. 'Most of the required business classes are filled, but I'll see what I can do.'"

'I don't care if I have to take basket weaving; I just have to get back in. I don't want to die.'

'I'll see what I can do.'

'Thank you, sir.'

"As I stood up to leave, he said, 'And Steve, our University doesn't offer a course in basket weaving.'"

'Yes sir.'

"A couple of days later, I had my admit slip and my list of classes. He got me into two Economics classes and Business Law, but the electives were brutal, Children's Lit and Ballroom Dancing. Not easy for a guy who can't keep a beat. I finished school three years later, and, by that time, the war was over."

"Well, whoever that adviser was, he sure saved your sorry ass," said Marty.

"Don't I know it," he said, wearing a shit-eating grin. "And what was your number?"

"It was three-forty-one. I literally won the lottery that night. What about you, Rob?"

"I wasn't so lucky. I was in my senior year of college in the middle of Kansas."

"Kansas? What the hell were you doing there?" asked Steve.

"When I got out of Bronx Community College,

some recruiter from the sunflower state offered me a scholarship. I thought it would be a good experience to leave the city for a few years. Plus, it was free!"

"Kansas, huh?"

From his back pocket, Rob took out a road map, folded it in quarters, and pointed to the middle crease. Newtown College in Newtown, Kansas, smack in the middle of the good old U S of A.

"You always carry a map with you?" I asked.

"Hey, you never know when you're going to need one."

Steve and I cracked up and Marty started choking on his booze.

Rob rambled on, "I watched the Vietnam lottery on TV in the dorm rec-room. There were about fifty guys there, mostly seniors, like me, and we were drinking and smoking and razzing each other all night long. When my birthday, February 14th, came up number four, the whole room got quiet. To relieve the tension, I blurted, 'How cold do you think it gets in Winnipeg in January?' Everyone laughed and the night went on, winners and losers, side by side, knowing that our lives had just changed forever. I looked into the Peace Corps, but there was a logjam of guys trying to get in. I applied for teaching jobs in underserved, remote areas, but when spring came around, I didn't have anything finalized yet. Then, three weeks before graduation, I got a notice from my draft board to report for my physical the following Wednesday. I was royally screwed."

"What did you do?" I asked.

Rob got up to pour a drink and I used this moment to reflect. I had always felt a little guilty for not serving. How unfair was it that a boy's future was arbitrarily determined by picking a number out of a hat? That's so random. But life is like that, isn't it? A crapshoot. A roll of the dice. Sometimes you win, sometimes you don't.

Fresh drink in hand, Rob went on. "I talked to my buddies who told me to go see Carson and Sweat, two super seniors who lived off campus and failed their physicals the year before. I'd met Sweat once at a keg party. He was a huge Hungarian guy about six-foot-five and weighed about two-fifty. He used to play football at Kansas State but was thrown off the squad for fighting with his teammates. He had these wild eyes, and, rumor had it, he and his buddy Carson had an LSD lab in their basement. At this point, I was desperate. So that afternoon, I hopped into my bug and drove over to their place. There I was, standing at the front door of a farmhouse at the end of a dirt road about five miles from campus. I couldn't find a doorbell, so I knocked a few times until an older lady with a gravelly voice asked what I wanted—only it came out 'whatchewwant'?

"An old lady?" I asked. "What the hell."

"Yeah, it shocked the shit out of me too. I told her I was looking for Sweat and she opened the door to me. Big smelly non-filtered cigarette in her mouth, she was puffing like a steam engine. I nearly choked from the smoke. She asked if I was from back east and I told her I was from New York City. She tells me to be careful with 'dem guys' because 'dem's fucken crazy' so I strolled around to the back, jumping over piles of beer cans and other shit and stepped up to a purple door, which someone had attacked with a spray can of day-glow paint. There was a peace sign somewhere on there, hidden under other graffiti like *Kill The Pigs* and

Make Wine Not War."

"I had a bumper sticker that said that," Marty said with a chuckle.

"Through an open window, I heard Commander Cody's voice on the stereo complaining about a hot-rod roadster and, as I knocked on the door, I swear I saw the upstairs curtain move before someone started down. The door opened and there stood Sweat, in a clean white bathrobe with the logo of the Hotel Conrad Chicago. He invited me in like I was a long-lost buddy."

"What did you do then?" Steve asked.

"I followed him into the house and all of a sudden in walked a skinny guy wearing a blue sports coat, gray pants, and white shirt with a green, paisley tie."

"Paisley ties. Remember those?" Marty asked. "I still have a few."

"No surprise there," Steve jeered. "Probably hanging next to your flowered pants."

"Hey, you never know. They may come back in style."

Rob continued with his saga. 'Sweat introduced the new guy as Carson, and damned if he didn't look exactly like Johnny Carson. I stood there dumbfounded, as they offered me a longneck out of an ancient refrigerator and asked what I needed. I told them I was scheduled for my draft physical on Wednesday with a Doctor Crowley in Wichita. Sweat called him Drowsy Crowley and said he always looked like he was asleep or in bad need of a nap. After going through the particulars, Carson gave me a couple of capsules and told me to take them exactly ninety minutes before my appointment. I asked why and he explained that they'd make my heart rate and blood pressure go sky-high, I'd feel cold as ice and then start to shiver. He told me the pills mimic epilepsy, but, if the doc asked, to play dumb."

"Were you nervous?" Steve asked.

Rob nodded. "As hell. I got to the medical building at half past twelve. I parked my car as far away as I could from the main entrance beneath a shady maple tree, unfolded the napkin with the two green pellets and forced them down with a long swig of orange soda. I sat there for about forty-five minutes trying to relax but found myself wide awake as I felt my heart start beating ridiculously fast. I stepped out of my car trying to take a short stroll but lost my balance and held on to the hood for support. I felt like I was in Jefferson Airplane's wonderland but couldn't figure out if I was the rabbit or the caterpillar."

"Why didn't you ask Alice?" cracked Steve, and we all started laughing.

"No seriously, this wasn't funny. I finally got my act together and discovered that by taking very small steps, I could manage to move my body forward without falling. It took me twenty minutes to walk the fifty yards to the front door, which luckily stood wide open."

"This is quite the story," said Steve. "You been taking lessons from Timbo?"

"No, no. Listen, will you?"

"Yeah, if I could stay awake."

"So, the receptionist eyed me suspiciously as she asked my name and date of birth and told me to take a seat and that the doctor would be with me shortly. There were three other guys in the waiting room, two wore uniforms of some sort and all had short hair. The office door opened and a huge Marine exited with a big smile on his face, and I remember thinking, he's probably just got a shot of penicillin to cure his bout with the clap. I started laughing and I couldn't stop until a pretty blonde nurse called my name and I followed her into a room with a couch, a small chair and a few machines. I don't really remember much of my exam because at that point everything was a blur. I started smiling when I first set my sights on Dr. Crowley, his eyes tiny slits that were likely to close any second. He did all the work and gave all the info to Nurse Blondie, who had the whitest teeth I'd ever seen. My blood pressure and my pulse were through the roof, like Sweat and Carson said, but at that point I was past the point of caring. All I wanted to do was hold open her mouth and check out those white pearls of hers. They were so beautiful. I barely managed to undress myself and was freezing cold as I stood there in my tightly-whiteys being poked in the belly like a little doughboy. Mercifully, the exam finally ended, the doctor left the room, and the nurse told me I was free to go and that I would get my results in a few days. I thanked her and tried to tell her she had a great smile, but I think I said, 'You have good tooth.' She gave me a really weird look. I went back to my car and sat in the front seat and closed my eyes. A security guard knocked on my window a few hours later, and I then drove back to my dorm and passed out on my bed."

"So," I asked, "when did you finally get the word?"

"A couple of days later, I got a letter in the mail telling me that I had failed the physical and had been classified by the US Army as 4F on the basis of *pes planus*. I didn't know what the hell that was, so I immediately took out my dictionary and looked it up. Nothing! I went across the hall to see this guy Benny, a real nerd and a pre-med major, thinking he could help me. Benny didn't like me much—a bit of a deal over a girl—so he just looked at me and said, 'It's flat feet, asshole.' I couldn't stop laughing. I soft shoed my precious footsies back to my room. Flat feet! Do you believe that shit? I went through five days of hell, when all I needed was a doctor's note saying I had flat feet!"

"So let's see those dogs," coaxed Marty, pouring everyone another splash.

Rob lifted his toes in the air and wiggled them around. "I was never the fastest guy on the block, but I wouldn't trade these puppies for all the tea in China."

"You mean Vietnam," said Steve.

We all laughed. "I wonder how different our lives would have been if we had served in that crazy war," I said.

"Well, we'll never know!"

"Amen to that," said Rob, as he raised his glass. "To Socket."

Chapter Nine

Around eleven the next morning, I jogged over to the gas dock, where we had tied up Socket's boat overnight. Three miles and forty minutes later, I hopped in his skiff, started the engine, and headed out to a mooring near his home. The wind let up as I entered the bay and made my way around Paradise Point to Corey Creek. There were many hidden sandbars, but Socket's small boat drew so little water that I easily found his buoy, secured the lines, and headed to the house. It was a summer bungalow with a screened-in porch and a shaky ladder that led to an upstairs loft. Back in the 1950s there were many such cottages in town. On weekends, families would drive or take the train from the big city for some sea and fresh air. Over the years, most of these old tinderboxes have been knocked down or renovated, and replaced by larger, more modern homes.

As I walked up the driveway, I noticed the side door was wide open. "Helloooo," I sang, stepping over the threshold.

"Is that you Timbo?" asked a familiar voice.

"Hey, Rob. What are you doing here?"

"I figured that I'd stop by, you know, just to make sure everything was locked up. There's some stuff in the refrigerator that we should toss before it goes bad."

"Actually, we need to be restocking the fridge, not cleaning it," I informed him. "Socket's niece is coming this weekend and she'll need a place to stay."

"Oh."

"So, cut the bullshit. You were looking for Socket's weed, weren't you?"

"Guilty as charged," he said with a smile, raising his hands up in the classic surrender pose. "I've been searching this place for an hour and can't find any sign of his plants."

"That's because he didn't grow it here. Too obvious. Everyone in town knew he grew his own pot, but the cops didn't bother him because he never sold any of it. He made just enough for his own use and, occasionally, he gave away a joint or two to friends."

I went to the kitchen sink, turned on the tap, and filled a Flintstones jelly glass with water. I strolled over to the brick fireplace, saddled on both sides with floor to ceiling books.

"I didn't know Socket was such a big reader," noted Rob.

"Yeah, he spent a lot of the winter in the library."

I glanced at his collection, impressed by the variety. Biographies of Teddy Roosevelt, Winston Churchill and JFK rested alongside historical novels like *Captain From Castile* and *Northwest Passage*. On a shelf all by themselves were the classic, nautical themed texts. Among them were some of my very own favorites, including *Moby Dick, Robinson Crusoe* and *The Perfect Storm*. While I looked over the titles, my buddy obsessively looked around for other things.

"Rob," I yelled, "read my lips. There is nothing here! Socket's plants could be anywhere from here to Orient Point. But they definitely are not here. A few years back, the old police chief tried unsuccessfully to find Socket's pot farm. But Socket was on to the cops and took them on these wild goose chases all the time. He knew the North Fork waters better than anyone. In fact, he once took his clam boat out during a ferocious nor'easter with the wind blowing sixty miles an hour. But he didn't care. He just laughed when the police cruiser following him almost capsized."

"Now let's get going. I got to get home to mow the grass."

He looked dejected. Like the keeper flounder he thought he was bringing up just turned into a horseshoe crab. I turned to him. "Rob, why are you so fixated on Socket's pot?"

"It makes me happy, and it eases the pains."

"The pains."

"Yeah, you know? The getting old junk like the joints, the muscles and the other stuff," he said, making his way out the door.

"What other stuff?"

Rob sat down on a wooden rocking chair. He took off his glasses and stared into space. "I can't believe Socket's gone. You never know when your number's up. Do you? he asked.

I made my way to the porch and sat next to him. I could tell he wanted to talk. I waited for him to continue.

"You know, when Sue retired from her job in the summer of 2001, her dream was to go on a vacation without any crowds. The only time teachers, like her, could take time off was in the summer or Christmas or spring break when all the kids had off too. Everyplace we went was mobbed and ridiculously expensive. So that September, I booked us for a ten-day honeymoon package in Bermuda. On the first Friday after Labor

Day, I said goodbye to all my cronies at the firehouse and the next morning Sue and I boarded a flight. Three days later, I was sitting on the beach, enjoying a Bloody Mary when the first plane hit the twin towers."

"Holy shit. I didn't know."

"Yeah. Some things you just don't talk about. Three hundred and forty-three firemen died that day. I would have been working that shift."

"Wow."

"The day after I returned from vacation, I handed in my retirement papers." He turned to me. "What about you. Where were you that morning?"

"Flying from New York to Washington DC."

"No shit."

"After I landed, I got into my rental car about 8:30 and was listening to the DJ rant about an idiot pilot crashing into the World Trade Center. Then the second one hit and I knew we were in trouble. I pulled over and immediately tried to get in touch with Catey, who worked in the city, but there was no service. I was a wreck. About two hours later she finally got through to me. I was never so relieved. I was so scared that something had happened to her."

"I can't imagine."

"As you know, all flights in the country were cancelled and the bridges into and out of New York were closed. I was stuck in the DC area, which was going through their own shit at the Pentagon. I was lucky that I had a rental car and a hotel room already booked so I spent the next few days just going through the motions. When they opened the bridges on Thursday afternoon, I headed home. The roads were empty and the tollbooths on the turnpike and bridges were free and manned by cops checking IDs and searching the backseats of cars. There were no lights on any of the roads that evening and from the top level of the Verrazzano, I could see smoke rising from the remains of those two buildings. I dropped off my rental at the airport and had to walk about two miles in the dark to get to my car. I finally pulled into my driveway about nine and was hugged tightly by a crying Catey. I just broke down."

Just then, our man-moment was interrupted by a truck pulling into the driveway.

"Shit," I muttered. "It's that jerk, Joey Wizkowski."

"Who's he?"

"Just some townie. Used to be a cop."

"Is he retired, too?"

"Not by choice. He spent nineteen years on the force but six months before he could collect his pension, he was thrown off under suspicious circumstances. Joey has been kicked out of every bar and restaurant in town. He's loud, obnoxious and a nasty drunk."

"Sound's like you know him pretty well."

"He lived a few blocks away from us before his wife caught him messing around and threw his sorry ass out of the house. He has a son who's now a cop in Florida. After graduating from high school, he moved down south and hasn't been back since. No love lost there."

The former cop sat behind the wheel of an old green pickup. We walked towards him and tapped on the passenger side window. "Hey Officer Wiz, what are you doing here?" I asked.

He hated the name Officer Wiz, so I made sure to call him that whenever we met.

"Hey," he said nervously. "I'm just making sure everything is okay for an old friend. I'm doing private security these days; Socket and I were pretty close a few years back, so I thought I would check on things. People hear about old guys dying and they try to take advantage of the situation. You know what I mean?"

"Oh, I know ex-act-ly what you mean."

"Is that what you're doing here too, taking care of things?"

Before I could answer, Joey's cell phone rang. He looked down, saw the caller ID, and blew me off. "I gotta go. It's too bad about Socket; we used to be real close, back in the day."

"So you say," I muttered as he rolled up the window and backed the truck down the driveway.

Word on the street was that on the night of the nor'easter, Officer Wiz was driving the police cruiser when it ended up in the drink. After his chief heard what the Wiz was up to, he went ballistic. Wiz had run the boat aground, twice, smashed it into the rocks by Brick Cove and shattered its windshield. How the hell do you break a boat windshield? It cost almost ten grand to repair the cruiser. Six months later, Officer Wiz resigned from the police force. Coincidence? I think not.

"What do you think he was doing here?" asked Rob.

"Same as you, my friend. Looking for gold. Socket's Gold."

Chapter Ten

Socket's roots were in farming. His dad had taught him how to graft trees and cross-pollinate plants in order to strengthen them against disease and help them produce new variants. After Socket came back from 'Nam, he put this know-how to good use by crossbreeding his own strain of marijuana.

His first big break came with Panama Haze, a hybrid that combined Panama Red and Neville's Haze, a huge hit when passed around at one very memorable Jimmy Buffet concert. As legend went, that same night was when Socket decided to get out of dealing and go into sharing. He said that he didn't need the money. His house was paid for and he had a few bucks in the bank. He always joked that fishing, clamming and friends in high places were enough to keep him happy.

A few years later, Socket took the Panama Haze and grafted it with a real mellow strain of weed called Stargazer. He called this new variety Ho Chi Wow to commemorate, or, as he joked, to commiserate, his days in Vietnam. And wow, spectacular it was!

Even more spectacular these days, now that pot was legal, was the chunk of change a mix like Ho Chi Wow could rake in.

Chapter Eleven

The following morning, Friday, Socket's niece Allison drove up from Philadelphia. She was a tall, thin woman with straight dark hair and looked to be in her mid-forties. As a single mom with two daughters in college, she needed this interruption from her accounting job like she needed another husband—and she'd already had two.

Marty met Allie at the hospital where they viewed the body and made the necessary arrangements. A memorial was planned for Monday afternoon at Founder's Landing. Marty and Pam invited her to dinner that evening and asked Catey and me to join them. When we got there, Allie was taking her first sip of sauvignon blanc.

"Come on in," said Marty. "Let me make the introductions. I don't know if you've ever met Socket's, I mean John's, niece Allison."

"It's okay, Marty," she said. "People have been calling Uncle Johnny, Socket, since I've known him. He was actually proud of the nickname."

"We are very sorry for your loss," said Catey.

"I'm just glad he left us without pain. He never totally recovered from his stint in Vietnam. I don't think he's had a good night's sleep in fifty years."

While Marty topped off Allison's glass and started to uncork the bottle of cab we brought over, Catey turned to Allie, "Any thoughts on what you're going to do with Socket's house?"

"I'm going to put it on the market, but I don't think I'll get much money out of the deal."

"You'd be surprised how much these little bungalows near the water are going for today."

"Yeah, but Uncle Johnny's house is really owned by the bank. About twenty years ago, he took out one of those reverse mortgages that must be paid back first. Besides, a lot of his money went to medical bills. After all is said and done, I'll be lucky if I have enough to buy dinner."

"Well, let's hope it's dinner at the Ritz," I joked.

"So how are your daughters Kim and Laura doing?" asked Marty, smoothly changing the subject.

"Very well. I'm impressed you remembered their names."

Marty snuck me a look and continued. "Socket loved those girls. Talked about them all the time. They both go to Penn State, right?"

"That's right. Kim is majoring in economics and Laura is into marine biology. I guess she takes after Uncle Johnny."

Pam walked into the dining room carrying a huge bowl. "I hope you like shrimp and grits."

We sat down to eat and raised our glasses once again to toast Socket.

"Uncle Johnny didn't have many friends. He was never very outgoing, and after he was discharged, he became even more of a loner. But he always felt comfortable around you guys."

"He was a good man, Allison," said Marty.

"Please, call me Allie."

Just then, Allie's cell phone started blasting a Cindy Lauper tune about girls having fun. She quickly shut it off. "Excuse me," she slurred, after taking a sip from her third glass of wine. "Do you guys know someone named Joey Wiz-something?"

"Yeah, Wizkowski," I answered. "He's a local. Why do you ask?"

"I don't know how he got my number, but he called me this morning. Said he was a good friend of Uncle Johnny's and wanted to express his sympathies. Is he a friend of yours?"

"Not really. But he and Socket had a relationship, of sorts. Joe used to be a policeman, but now he does some kind of security work."

"When we spoke, I told him about the memorial, so I guess I'll meet him on Monday."

Marty and Pam got up to clear the table.

"So" Allie asked, "how do you guys know Uncle Johnny?"

"Mostly from fishing," I said, "but the first time I met him was in the middle of the bay."

"Really?"

"Tim and I didn't always live on the water," explained Catey. "Thirty years ago we bought a tiny summer cottage down the road. And, before we even signed the contract," she went on, looking straight at me, "someone decided that he needed a boat."

"Hey, wait a minute," I interrupted. "You can't live close to the water without a boat. Just ask Lyle Lovett. Besides, I got us a great deal. A 1970, seventeen-foot bow rider with a 90-horsepower engine. We got the boat, the trailer and a mooring all for under a thousand bucks. It was a steal!"

"Yeah, a real bargain, except for two things. We lived an hour away from here and we were clueless when it came to trailering a boat."

Allie's cell phone started vibrating. She looked down at the number and ignored the call.

Catey continued, "So on the first sunny day that May, we started our fifty-mile trek to Southold, pulling a boat loaded with a two-hundred-pound mooring and all of this guy's fishing stuff."

"We even had a queen size mattress tied to the roof," I added.

"Yeah, and in the back seat, asleep in his booster, squeezed in between the boxes, was our three-year-old son, Kevin, being licked by our six-month-old puppy, Rover."

"I was smart enough to let Catey drive," I smiled.

"I never did thank you for that, did I, honey?"

Allie laughed and took another sip. "Please, don't stop now."

"When we got to the boat ramp, I jumped on the deck of my ship, as Catey flawlessly backed up the boat and trailer into the bay. I unclipped the bow and tied a line to a post next to the ramp. Success! Catey pulled the truck and trailer away from the water and got out with Kevin and the dog to wave goodbye. All of a sudden, she watched, stunned, as water started rushing into the hull.

"Oh shit, I think I'm sinking," I shouted out to her.

"Catey looked at me, then at Kev, then at Rover and yelled, 'Sorry, but you're on your own now.'"

"It was our first boat fight. Luckily, I found the switch to the bilge pump and the water started to recede. I had forgotten to install my boat's plug."

"Which was in the pocket of his shorts," winked Catey, making us all laugh.

Allie's phone lit up again, but she paid it no attention.

"So, anyway, I motored my way into the bay. I felt so cool, you know, like Humphrey Bogart on the *African Queen*, until boom. I found myself stuck on a huge sandbar. I'd probably still be there if Socket hadn't shown up."

"That's where you met him?" asked a surprised Allie.

"Yeah. He thought I was clamming. When I told him I was stuck and trying to get to Duck Creek, he laughed his ass off. Taking out his chart to show me where we were, he said he had never met anyone trying to go over an island with a boat. I think he felt sorry for me when he heard it was my first time in these waters. He just smiled, shook his head, and told me to follow him. So I did, and we've been friends ever since."

Marty and Pam returned to the table just as Allie's phone started buzzing again. She took another glance at the screen. "This guy just won't give up. I wonder what he wants now."

"Who?" asked Catey.

"That Joe Wiz-guy."

Marty and I just stared at each other.

Chapter Twelve

Saturday morning dawned bright and sunny with a strong northeast wind threatening to keep the temperature low. As every fisherman knows, *"When the wind blows from the east, the fishing is the least."* So, after my morning jellyfish, I kayaked to my favorite spot, dreaming of steamed clams for dinner.

Morning kayak rides are always special, but the quiet of that particular daybreak had me mulling about Socket. He had me by almost six years, but I never thought of him as old. He was one of us, not ancient like my childhood neighbors. Mr. Anderson, on the right, was a retired accountant who loved to garden; he taught me how to prune bushes, plant flowers and pull weeds. On the other side was Charlie.

Charlie lived with a heavy-set woman named Helen, thirty years his junior, who might have been his wife, niece, lover, or all of the above. He was a nocturnal creature who often roamed his yard at three in the morning, clipping hedges, mowing the lawn or raking leaves, behavior that the neighbors graciously accepted as normal.

But to us kids, Charlie was a bit scary. He always wore a red plaid CPO shirt and a long billed woolen cap— even in the dog days of summer. My friends and I suspected that he was kinda like the Johnny Rivers guy, a Russian spy delivering coded messages to other secret agents in the neighborhood. We watched as each morning he left the house wheeling a rusty shopping cart to places unknown. One day, we followed the old man only to find him scrounging the local fruit markets searching for the perfect peach or plum. Another time, he offered us a piece of bubblegum that we reluctantly accepted, though we had no idea how we would split it up. He must have realized we were only being polite because he smiled a toothless grin and uttered kindly in some foreign language that I later learned was Polish.

Late one August afternoon, a police car pulled up next door, and I saw Helen crying hysterically. My mom ran over to comfort her and told us later that Charlie and his shopping cart had been T-boned by a station wagon. During dinner that night, my parents lamented the fact that Charlie had never recovered from the war. Listening to them, I felt sad but confused. Recovered how?

Looking back now, I get it. I ask myself if Charlie was happy or if he was just biding his time? What made him get up every morning? Was it Helen or simply the start of each new day? I still wonder if he checked out on his own terms. I guess I'll never know. Life is a mystery, precious, especially if you love and are loved.

Suddenly, Catey's face popped up on my phone, nudging me back to reality. "Clams for dinner?" she asked, hope in her voice.

"Afraid not."

"No problem. How 'bout we do the triathlon?"

"Sounds like a plan."

That afternoon we kayaked across the bay, hiked up to Founders Pub, and took a seat at the bar. Lucy came right over and placed two cold beers in front of us. An expert bartender with a happy-go-lucky flair that made everyone comfortable, she remembered the names and quirks of her regulars and was up to date on all the gossip in our small town.

As Catey and I were finishing our burgers and our last round, we watched Lucy reach up for an artsy shaped bottle of expensive tequila.

I whistled. "Who's that for?"

"Officer Wiz," she whispered. "He's been pouring on the charm all afternoon for some new lady-friend. I think it's Socket's niece."

I just shook my head.

Chapter Thirteen

Next morning, the weather was perfect for fishing. I texted the boys and got the thumbs up. By ten o'clock we were in my boat looking for fluke, again.

"I need a few fish before the Fourth," announced Marty. "I promised the kids tacos."

"I don't know. Not much action," muttered Steve, his mouth full of chocolate. "Maybe they moved to Montauk."

"Not this one," I hollered, reeling in a giant sea robin.

"It's a bird," yelled Rob, "and a big one. Ugly too. Look at those bulging eyes on the top of its head."

"Why do they call them birds?" asked Marty.

"Check out their fins," pointed Steve. "They're so far away from their bodies that they look like they're flying instead of swimming."

All of sudden the fish started yapping.

"He's barking," said Marty. "Can you eat these suckers?"

"Yeah," I interjected, "but there's only two strips of real meat. The rest is bones. It's not worth it. It's like killing a bull for its balls."

"Ever eat Rocky Mountain oysters?" asked Steve.

Marty made a face.

"Don't knock them till you try them, especially with a cold beer."

"Speaking of which, who needs one?" he asked.

"There's plenty in the cooler," I said. "Help yourselves."

"Chocolate with a chaser of beer. And it's not even noon. Doesn't get any better than this."

"Reminds me of my college days," said Rob. "I had a roommate, junior year, who was a real stud. He would come back from some girl's dorm at the crack of dawn, pop open a can, and boast about his latest conquest."

"I hated guys like that," said Steve.

"He was a rich, preppy type, dressed straight out of *GQ*, and the chicks were all over him."

"Any of them rub off on you?" asked Marty.

"No such luck!" lamented Rob.

"So when was the first time you got laid?"

"I had a girlfriend during my first year of junior college. I would spend Tuesday afternoons at her house studying, hmm, her anatomy. That's where I sealed the deal."

"How about you, Steve?"

"I was young, about sixteen. I went surfing with this girl over Easter vacation. The water was freezing, so I got out, took off my wetsuit and hopped into the van. And so did Melinda. I'll never forget those twenty seconds of sheer bliss."

"How about you, Marty?" asked Steve, reaching for another beer.

"Pam and I met when we were sixteen. One night, after a year of serious dating, I snuck into her room, and we did it to a Righteous Brothers melody.

"The Righteous Brothers," proclaimed Rob. "The musical mezcal of the sixties."

"Don't laugh. It still works—if you got that loving feeling," added Marty. "Hey Timbo, you're pretty quiet over there. What gives?"

"Nothing."

"Oh, come on. Spill."

"Okay, if you must know, I was the king of second base. Spent more time there than Willie Randolph. Felt more tits and juggled more boobs than a circus performer. Every time I'd try for third, something would come up."

"I could guess what that was."

"No, well, yes. But remember, I went to a Catholic college with a bunch of holy rollers saving it for when they got married. Remember what Billy Joel sang about them?"

"Don't tell me Catey was your first."

"No, no. I was at a friend's wedding upstate. I was doing shots with this hot bridesmaid. Next morning, I woke up in her room, in her bed, naked. I think I had a happy ending, but, truthfully, I can't remember."

Steve stuffed another sweet in in his mouth. "Sounds like the perfect date to me. He didn't even have to pay for dinner."

"Hold up. I got something," yelled Marty.

"What is it?"

"It feels like, a ahhh shit, my back!"

Marty went down quickly. He lay on the boat cushions wincing in pain. His face was bone white and he was sweating like he had just run a marathon.

"Let's get him home," I said. "He ain't looking so good."

"Doesn't sound so good either."

"Marty, what do you need?"

"Booze?"
"Weed?"
"How 'bout a chocolate bar?"

Chapter Fourteen

Socket's memorial was held on a beautiful summer day. Seventy-five degrees, no clouds, and a breeze slight enough to keep the mosquitoes away. The perfect afternoon for kayaking over to Founders Landing. When Pam, Marty, Catey and I pulled up to the beach, a conga line of people were already shaking Allie's hand, giving her hugs, and expressing their sympathy. After about an hour, an old army chaplain stood up, said a prayer and read a eulogy. Father Ben was a big man who put everyone at ease with his signature joke about being old and overweight. "The longer I get around, the rounder I get." His was a good sermon about Socket's love of the water, people, fishing and clamming. After the speech, Allie slowly walked down to the shore, alone, took off her sandals and ceremoniously scattered Socket's ashes into the sea.

As the guests milled about, Catey and I were behind a makeshift bar serving drinks. Out of the corner of my eye, I spotted Officer Wiz, arriving unfashionably late. Overly dressed in gray slacks, blue blazer and a red striped tie, he sheepishly approached Allie. She walked away. When he made his way to the bar, I blurted out, perhaps a little bit too loud, "Hey, Officer Wiz, you finally made it. I was wondering when you were going to show up."

"Hi, Tim," he slurred. "Can I get a vodka and soda?"

Despite his fancy digs, he looked a bit disheveled,

and his eyes were glazed over.

"Sorry Wiz. We only serve beer, wine and soda at this establishment."

"Then, just give me a glass of seltzer," he said, opening his jacket to show off a silver flask.

I filled a red solo cup with soda water, tossed in a lime for good luck, and handed it to him. "Classy move, Wiz, bringing your own booze to a memorial."

He walked away but not before he gave me a scowl. Someone beside me blurted, "What an asshole."

I turned and there stood my fishing buddy Rob and his wife Sue. I shook his hand and gave his bride a hug. They were an odd twosome. She was a sharp clotheshorse while he was fashionably challenged. Today she wore black leggings, a silk tunic with a bright yellow ascot and a straw hat. Rob wore his usual outfit–tan cargo shorts, graphic tee shirt, blue baseball cap, and black high-tops.

"You look great," I said to Sue. "I see that your hubby here got all dolled up for the occasion." I looked at Rob. "Where's that one from?"

"Led Zeppelin."

"The stairs to heaven ticket? I get it," I said, offering up a fist bump.

Tenting his shirt from the bottom hem for everyone to see, Rob bragged, "Hey, this one's clean."

"Not for long," teased Sue. "I hear they're serving baked ziti."

"Then I'll just turn it inside out," he joked. "Hey, Tim, what kind of beer you got back there?"

"Regular or light, generously donated by the VFW."

Ginny and Steve walked up behind them. Steve had

on a lightweight Hawaiian print shirt, and Ginny's white sundress peeked out from under an oversized sweatshirt. They agreed to take over the bar for me.

I walked over to Allie. "How are you holding up?" I said, handing her a white wine.

"I was doing fine until that jerk Joe showed up, late and half in the bag."

"He's kind of an oddball," I said, trying to be nice, all the while noticing Wiz, standing alone, pouring another shot of vodka into his cup.

"I don't get it," Allie said. "He was so kind to me on Saturday. Came with me to pick up the urn and then even took me to dinner."

She stared at Wiz, who at the moment seemed to be checking out the catering chick. "Truth is we both probably had one drink too many, and when he took me home, I invited him in. Stupid, I know. I put on some music, but his eyes were everywhere but on me. Come to think of it, most of our conversation that night centered on my uncle."

"How so?" I asked, hoping for some kind of clue.

She shifted on her feet. "He kept asking questions about Johnny's clamming places and his secret fishing spots. Then, on my way back from the bathroom, I caught him rummaging through the kitchen drawers, claiming he was looking for a corkscrew. What the hell do you think he was really looking for?"

"Socket's pot, of course."

"You mean this?" she smiled, pulling a joint out of her purse and handing it to me.

"Exactly, except that's just the beginning." After a moment's hesitation, I said, "You may not have known this, Allie, but Socket grew his own pot and experimented with cross breeding different varieties. He came up with a few strains that could be worth some very serious money to certain people."

"You're kidding me. I knew Uncle Johnny liked his dope, but I never knew he grew it. Where was he doing that?"

"That, my dear, is the sixty-four-million-dollar question."

****

I never was a big fan of marijuana. I first tried the stuff the summer after high school. My friends and I were at a beach parking lot sitting on the hoods of our cars, Springsteen-like, drinking beer and shooting the breeze when somebody whipped out a joint. He lit it up and started passing it around, and when it came to me, I took a puff on it like I was the Marlboro Man.

"That's not gonna get you high," said my buddy Lloyd who was sitting next to me. Stick, on my other side, just laughed. "You've never smoked before, Timbo, have you?"

"No," I confessed.

I watched both of them demonstrate the how to. They took long drags and held the smoke in their lungs for a while. I followed their leads and passed the joint on. I didn't feel the effects of the pot at all, so when it came around my way again, I took another long toke. About five minutes later, I started grinning. Then, I remember my funny friend Mikey asking, "What do you call a deer without eyes?"

Stick thought for a moment. "Don't know."

"No eye deer."

Everyone laughed, except me.

Then Mikey asked, "What do you call a deer with

no eyes and no legs?"

A moment of silence followed.

"Still, no eye deer."

Then we all cracked up.

The next morning every bone in my body hurt. I vaguely remember laughing a lot, jumping off a lifeguard stand, skinny-dipping in the bay, and being slapped in the face by a girl.

My next experience with pot was a month later during freshman orientation. That didn't go so well either, so I swore off the stuff for good. I figured that my other vices, chain smoking and binge drinking, were enough to keep me busy so I didn't need the weed. These days, I mow the grass occasionally, sometimes with a lawn trimmer and sometimes with a pipe.

****

Once the dishes of food were laid out, Catey and I went back to work filling the mourners' plates with pasta. Then we set out coffee and dessert, emptied the trash, and packed up the leftovers. I saw Officer Wiz and Allie talking on the beach, and they seemed to have recovered from their spat. Both walked over, and he personally thanked Catey and me for helping Allie with the memorial. I shook his hand, but only because it felt like the right thing to do. They walked away toward the parking lot and separated after a quick embrace. The magic was gone.

After the majority of guests had left, I uncorked a bottle of cab for Catey and me. The rest of the gang moseyed over. The sun was just beginning to set, an orange halo escorting his majesty down for the evening as the eight of us sat down to watch the show. Allie joined us, buried her feet in the sand, and thanked all of us again for sharing the day. As we raised our cups to the waning sun, Marty stood and spoke to Socket one last time. "May you finally find peace, my friend."

"Amen."

"What a beautiful night," said Sue.

Reaching into my pocket, I grabbed the joint that Allie had given me, and winked at her. I struck a match to it, took a puff, and passed it on to Marty.

"This night just keeps getting betterer and betterer," he said, laughing and coughing at the same time.

"I smell wacky weed," whooped Rob, a smile the size of Staten Island crossing his face. He took a long drag and starting singing, off key as usual. "This is Socket's best stuff. Ho Chi Wow!"

What a sight we must have been, eight children of the sixties, sitting on a seawall, smoking dope, drinking wine and watching the sun set.

"Nope, it doesn't get any better than this," agreed Steve.

Suddenly, Neil Young came on the radio. Catey giggled, and the place went to hell. Pam tried to respond but lost her train of thought. Rob was searching his pockets for his roach clip. Marty got another bottle of vino and topped everyone off. Sue got up to sway to the music and Ginny joined her. I sat there and smiled as the harvest moon started to rise.

Steve asked to no one in particular, "Any baked ziti left?"

"Sorry," said Allie. "I gave it to the VFW guys, but there are a few bags of chips by the cooler."

He got up and came back with large bags of

pretzels and corn crisps.

As these were being passed around, Rob blurted out, "I bet pretzels are like snowflakes, no two alike."

Marty laughed, "No, like fingerprints," he said, waving his hands in the air.

We talked chips and ate crap for another hour until we couldn't see straight. I got up and pointed to the sky, "Hey Marty, check out that moon."

"Bella Luuuna," he howled as Catey leaned over and gave me a kiss.

Chapter Fifteen

Allie rang our doorbell at ten the next morning. She declined my invitation for coffee, saying she just wanted to say goodbye and thank us for all our help. Her plan was to return in a few weeks with her girls to clean out her uncle's house and have a yard sale.

The holiday weekend was approaching; Catey and I knew that the Fourth of July craziness was about to invade the North Fork. Traffic, fireworks and crowded beaches were things we locals learned to avoid. I spent my Tuesday puttering around the house and Catey drove west to food shop. Because a heat wave was forecast for the end of the week, Marty planned a fishing trip for the following day before the hot weather set in. Low tide was at eight, so we decided on a gentleman's start of ten o'clock.

That morning, when I showed up next-door, fishing pole in hand, Rob and Steve were just arriving. Within minutes, the four of us motored out to the Old Oyster Factory. We passed a lot of boats, early birds who fished the outgoing tide and were returning with their catch. We waved to the people on board and they returned the gesture.

"Why do boaters always wave to each other?" asked Rob. "Is it a special sign?"

"I think it means 'How's it going?' Everything's great.' and 'Who's got it better than us?' all rolled into one," I gloated.

"I think you're right," said Marty.

"How's the back?"

"It feels a little better. I slept on my side last night," he said, and, without missing a beat, added, "so now my shoulder hurts."

We commiserated before making our way to the targeted buoy, where we lowered our baited hooks and waited patiently for something to strike.

"I'd like to catch a keeper fluke today," said Marty. "I found this ceviche recipe in *The Times* that sounds incredible."

"What's in the recipe," I asked.

"Lots of stuff."

"What, you don't remember?"

"Sure do. One pound of fish—fluke or halibut—works best, two tablespoons lime juice, one teaspoon each of lemon and orange juice, a quarter cup of shallots and jalapeno peppers without the seeds, for taste."

"So, our memory drug is working, I see?"

"I guess so."

"It's amazing," interrupted Steve. "I'm remembering all kinds of stuff that I always used to forget. Last night we were watching Mel Brooks' *History Of The World* and Ginny asked me the actor's name."

"Out of the blue Gregory Hines came to mind, and I was right."

"Gregory Hines. Wasn't he a tap dancer or something?" asked Rob.

"Sounds like you been popping your jellies, too." I smiled.

"Yeah, but did you know," Marty blurted, "that Mel Brooks originally picked Richard Pryor for the part, until his hair caught on fire?"

"You remembered that?"

"No, I googled him, but give me credit for getting his name right."

"Fish on," yelled Steve. "It feels like a big one."

Marty moved to get out of Steve's way when something struck his bait too. I quickly gave my pole to Rob, grabbed the net, and scooped it under Steve's rod.

"Looks like a keeper," said Rob, as I dropped the fish on the deck and rushed to Marty's bent pole.

"This sucker feels huge," he said, continuing his slow battle with the flatty. A few minutes later, the fish finally reached the surface, saw the boat, shook its giant head and spit the hook right out of its mouth. Luckily, my net was strategically placed underneath and the fluke rested safely in my possession.

"Wow! That's a doormat," shouted Steve.

"Oh shit," yelled Rob. "I got a fish on both poles!"

I grabbed my rod from Rob and reeled up quickly. Marty's catch was still tangled in the net so Rob and I had to land our fish the old fashioned way; we got us two more keepers, though not nearly the size of Marty's or Steve's.

The next drift yielded two more large ones and three shorts. The third drift was fast with only one short, and soon the conversation turned to other subjects. We talked about Socket's memorial and Rob's ecstasy over his reacquaintance the other night with Ho Chi Wow.

We all had a few good laughs.

Rob felt a tug on his line and started reeling, but

there was little movement.

"Whatcha got?" I asked.

"I'm not sure. Whatever it is, it's nothing big," he moaned, pulling it over the rail.

"It's a blowfish," Steve said. "I haven't seen one of these in years."

"Just look at it," I gasped, suddenly nostalgic. "It's a thing of beauty."

"Are you kidding me? It looks prehistoric," said Marty. "Check out those huge shamrock eyes."

"He's got wings too," said Rob, fingering the translucent fins. "Let's call him Hootie."

We just groaned.

"Blowfish," I laughed. "I can remember going with my buddies to Zach's Bay for flounder, and all we pulled in were blowfish, after blowfish, after blowfish. We got dozens. My father loved to eat them, so I decided to take them home. On the way, at a red light, a nerdy senior from school pulled up next to us. I tossed one of the fish into the front seat of his hot rod Vega. 'Shotgun!' we yelled, laughing our asses off."

"That's what you get for keeping your passenger window down," cracked Rob.

"Back home, I watched my dad clean those suckers. It's really simple. You just cut off the head and put a notch in the belly and pull the skin right off. What's left looks like a chicken leg."

"That's why they call them the chicken of the sea," noted Steve.

"They're tasty, too. Just dredge the tail in flour, then egg-wash, then bread crumbs, add salt and pepper, and sauté in butter."

"Don't forget the garlic," said Steve.

"You're right, Irish mistake. The next day my dad fertilized his vegetable patch with the leftover fish parts and my backyard stunk for about a week. After a while the odor went away or I became immune to it, but that summer, my father had a bumper crop of lettuce, peppers and cucumbers. He was most proud of his tomatoes, which were huge, bordering on the size of grapefruits. Strangely, every time I took a bite of one, it tasted a little fishy."

"Your old man sounds like a character," said Steve.

"Oh he was."

"Old man," said Marty. "That phrase keeps popping up. Old man, this. Old man, that."

"Yeah. Old man. Old... man. Oh shit! Marty, we're so freaking stupid."

"What?"

"Marty, start the engine."

"Why? What's wrong, Timbo?"

"Just head to Socket's place."

"Now?" asked Rob.

"Just humor me."

Marty started the motor and headed over past Paradise Point to Corey Creek and beached the boat. I hopped out and tied a line to a nearby tree. "Come with me Marty. You guys mind the boat. We'll be back in a few."

"I'll start fileting the fluke," offered Rob.

"If I knew we were going hiking, I would've worn my sneakers," said Marty.

"The house is only a few blocks from here."

"Yeah, but this hill is killing my back."

Moments later, we retrieved the key and opened the door to a musty smell. I rushed into the living room and stared at the wall of books. Nestled between *The Sun Also Rises* and *A Farewell To Arms* stood a worn leather copy of *The Old Man and the Sea*. I pulled it from the shelf and quickly flipped through the pages to no avail. Finally, with a hand on both the front and back covers, I turned the book upside down and shook it. A small piece of paper about the size of a playing card floated to the floor.

Marty bent down, picked it up and turned to me. "It's just a piece of paper with a phone number on it."

"Shit! I was hoping for a treasure map."

Chapter Sixteen

Tired and sweaty, an out of shape Officer Wiz jogged up the hill to Socket's place. He had parked his truck a few blocks away. Now all he needed to do was to figure out how to get into the house. He decided to call Allie and pick her brain.

She answered on the third ring. "Hi Joe. How you doing today?"

"Oh, I'm doing fine. Just checking up on you, making sure you made it home okay."

"That's sweet. Everything's good here."

"Great. My business is kinda slow right now and I have lots of free time. I thought that if you needed any help getting rid of Socket's stuff, I'm available."

"I think I've got that covered. My girls are coming back with me next week and Uncle Johnny's friends are helping us with the yard sale. So thanks, but I'm okay. Wait a sec, will you? My boss just walked in."

While on hold, Officer Wiz heard voices coming from inside. He hid behind the shed and watched Marty and Tim exit the front door, place the key under the mat, and start walking down the hill.

Allie came back on the line. "Joe, I'm really busy. Gotta go. Bye." And with that, the connection was gone.

Officer Wiz slowly walked back to the house and grabbed the key from its hiding place. He started searching, meticulously combing each room, opening every drawer and cabinet, looking for a clue to Socket's stash. What he didn't know is that the only thing of value had already been taken.

****

Hiking downhill, Marty and I were renewed with energy.

"So did you find anything?" asked Steve once we got to the boat.

"Nothing important," said Marty. "Just this piece of paper with a phone number on it.

"Should we call it?"

"It could lead us to Socket's leaves of grass," I said.

"Nobody laughed."

"Where did you find it?" asked Steve.

"Fittingly, in a Hemingway book, a place you illiterates would never look," I sneered.

"Was it *The Old Man and the Sea*? I read that one; It was only a hundred pages."

"Because you had to," cracked Marty.

"We all did," said Rob. "Thank goodness for cheat sheets."

I pulled out my cell and made the call. After five rings, a female voice answered. "Via Pizza, please hold."

Holding my phone away from my mouth, I whispered, "Via Pizza."

"A pizza joint?" asked Steve, all of a sudden very excited. "Is it close by?"

"I don't know yet."

After a few minutes, the voice returned to the line. "Sorry about the wait. What can I get you?"

"I'd like to speak to the owner, please."

"It's lunchtime. Call back later." Click.

"What was that about?"

"The owner was busy, so I have to call back."

Steve started googling the place. After a couple of seconds, he moaned, "Figures. Fifty-five Main Street, Mystic, Connecticut. I was hoping they were local. Just listen to these reviews. Five stars from Tripadvisor and *The New London Day* calls it 'The best slice in eastern Connecticut.'"

"Hey," said Rob. "Mystic isn't far, only a few exits north of where the ferry docks."

Steve stared at us, a pleading look in his eyes. "Anybody up for a road trip?"

Chapter Seventeen

Typical for July, the weather started to get hot and humid, and our ambitions waned as the sweat factor rose. Another few weekends came and went, and with the rise in water temperature, the fishing in our area came to a halt. When black sea bass season opened on August first, the bait shop reported some big catches in the Long Island Sound, so we decided to leave the comfort of our local bays.

Black sea bass is an oblong-shaped fish with a large mouth full of sharp teeth. The prickly spines on its back and dorsal fin make it difficult to hold in one's hands, and its black eyeball surrounded by red trim is quite scary. The consistency of the white, flaky meat is firm, and it tastes best when scaled and cooked whole in the oven or on a grill. Last year, Catey and I tried it raw as sashimi, and it was delicious.

With temperatures in the nineties and a chance of thunderstorms, we decided to fish off Steve's boat because it had the most shelter just in case the weathermen were right. We met at his dock at eight, knowing we had to navigate around the northern tip of the island and through the dangerous waters of Plum Gut, a forty-five-minute trip in good weather.

The sky was cloudy and the water tranquil when we launched, but within ten minutes, a dark cloud threatened, and the weather turned to shit. Once the waves started to lap over our bow, we decided to ditch the boat in Greenport and wait the storm out at the

Coronet, a small local coffee shop known for its corned beef hash. We high tailed it into the café, grabbed a table, and sat down to hot coffee and the hungry man's special.

"We just made it," said Rob. "Wouldn't want to ruin my Metallica shirt."

"Afraid it might rust?" joked Steve.

We groaned.

"Hey, Timbo, you okay?" Rob asked. "You're real quiet this morning."

"I'm just tired, I guess. Didn't sleep well; woke up too late to have coffee. Still waiting for things to percolate if you catch my drift."

The waitress came by and refilled our mugs. "This should help," I said, raising my cup in the air. "Truth is, I'm still unnerved by a recurring nightmare that I had last night."

"A nightmare?" asked Rob.

"The sixty-nine dream."

"That's not a dream. It's a fantasy," he smiled.

"No.The dying at sixty-nine dream."

"The what?"

"The turning seventy dream. If you die on the day before your seventieth birthday, people will go to your funeral and say, 'He was young, only in his sixties. How sad.'"

"Huh?"

"Yeah, if you last one more day, people at your wake will say, 'He was seventy. He had a pretty good run.'"

"So, is it better to die at sixty-nine or seventy?" asked Rob. "I don't get it."

"You're an ass," said Steve. "There's never a good

time to die."

"I don't know about that," I interjected. "To accomplish something really great, something good for mankind, might be a good trade off to a short life. History worships the Joan of Arcs and Martin Luther Kings. Maybe there's something to it."

"Hell, look at Buddy Holly and Hendrix," said Rob.

"If you guys keep extolling the virtues of dying young," said Marty, "then I'm ordering more bacon."

"Well, you got plenty of time," said Steve. "My radar app says things look pretty bad. If we're lucky, we may get a break in a half hour, but, after that, they're talking cats and dogs."

"Raining cats and dogs," said Rob. "Never understood that either."

"It's Greek. Look it up."

"Speaking of cats, there's that cat boat again," muttered Marty.

"You talking to yourself?"

He pointed out the window.

"You mean that boat? The blue one?" I asked.

"Yeah, that's a Global Cat, very unique. It has dual hulls like a catamaran and the beam is about a foot wider than most boats. I test-drove it. It's real comfortable, with plenty of room. Almost bought it, except for one thing."

"Not pricey enough, rich boy?" kidded Steve.

"Very funny. No, it drew too much water."

"You know, last week, that same boat followed Catey and me. We were looking for one of her pickle-ball friend's place in Orient Harbor. We drove around Long Beach Bay checking out houses and the whole time this boat was on our tail. At first, I thought it might be a harbormaster, but there were no markings on the hull. He was still riding our wake when we headed out to Bug Light, so Catey floored it and left him in the dust."

"Yeah. I saw him, too," Steve said. "Yesterday, when I was getting gas. This big guy with a floppy hat and sunglasses. Riding my ass. Strange, it's as if he was stalking me."

Chapter Eighteen

Alone and grumpy, Officer Wiz could hardly keep his eyes open. "Why the hell do they have to fish so early?" he yelled out to no one. "Tailing these boats is a royal pain in my ass. And now it's starting to rain. What the fuck else can go wrong?"

A bolt of lightning flashed nearby.

"Shit, shit, shit," he mumbled, as he motored to the nearest pier to tie up. He was huddled under the boat's T-top to keep dry when his cell phone rang. He glanced at the number and smiled. "Hello?"

"Hey, Joey. It's JT. How's it going?"

"Not too good today. I'm on a boat, stuck in the rain."

"It's too bad you're not upstate with me. It's beautiful here in God's country. I'm sitting on my back deck overlooking the farm, and all I see for miles is corn, soybeans and sunflowers. And the money crop gets planted in the spring."

JT, Officer Wiz's oldest friend from the neighborhood, now owned a hemp farm in the Hudson Valley. "Sounds fuckin' wonderful, JT."

"So what made you get another boat? Still cruising chicks at your age?"

"It's not my boat. I just look after it for some doctor. One of the rich "citiots" who discovered the North Fork."

"Ha-ha. We haven't talked in a dog's age. You still with Sally?"

"Nah. We split up."

"No shit. What happened?"

Joe took off his sunglasses and wiped the rainwater from his eyes. "The usual. We just stopped getting along."

"That's too bad. She get the house?"

"She got fucking everything."

"She still around?"

"No. She's living west of here. Shacked up with her personal trainer. I think he's jacked up on steroids."

"If he's as bulked up as you say he is, his balls are probably the size of a peanut."

"Ha-ha."

"She get her mitts on your pension, too?"

"No. I never got in my twenty. The chief and I didn't get along, so I got out a few years back."

"So, whatcha doing now?"

"I got a PI license and I'm a security consultant."

"Joey Wiz, private eye. Sounds pretty cool. You got a hot secretary who answers the phone and makes coffee?"

"No such luck. It's not like the movies. Actually, it's pretty boring. Right now, I'm chasing after some country club clowns, who as soon as it started drizzling, ducked into a cozy breakfast joint. And now I'm stuck here getting soaked." Joe held onto his hat as a gust of wind blew across the bow.

"Sure sounds like you could use a toke of my stuff."

"Probably, but I wouldn't take that chance. Remember Ed Barkley from high school?"

"Yeah, he played hoops with you."

"He's the new chief here in Southold. I just got hired for the summer on a temporary basis. I think I got a shot at getting back permanently."

"Cool. How's your son? What's his name again?"

"Ryan. He's down in Florida, working as a cop."

"A chip off the old block. So what's up Joey? Why'd you call the other day?"

"Do you remember a guy named Socket?"

"Socket, Socket. It rings a bell."

"Tall, skinny guy. Always wore an army coat."

"Oh yeah. The guy that got shot in 'Nam. Isn't he the one with the wicked weed?"

"Actually, that's why I called. He died, and I might be the beneficiary of some of his stash!"

"You're shitting me. When?"

"I'm working on it."

"Call me when you get your hands on the goods, and we'll work out a deal—all cash!"

"Fuckin' A."

Chapter Nineteen

The clouds disappeared, the sun was hot, and the boat was drying fast, so after breakfast we started back. Since nobody had any plans for the day, Steve shut down the engine, turned on the radio, and we drifted.

I put on my sunglasses as a lazy summer number by the Kinks started playing on the radio, and I thought to myself, "Isn't it amazing that certain songs always come up just at the right time?"

Steve took off his shirt to apply sunscreen and announced with gusto, "And once again, the weatherman is wrong."

"That's nothing new," said Marty. "I say get rid of all the weathermen. We just need weather *girls!*"

"Yeah, hot ones under thirty-five," panted Rob, carving hourglass shapes in the air.

"And they all have to wear low-cut tops and mini skirts. And when they hit thirty-five, ship them out on assignment to cover hurricanes and tornadoes," added Marty.

"I have a friend who's obsessed with the weather girls in South America," said Steve. "Single, never married, goes by the name Bucky. He sends me lots of videos, but I'm scared shitless to open most of them because I'm sure they're full of viruses. But the other day, when I saw *Weathergirls from Brazil* on my screen, I couldn't resist. These girls are so hot, prancing around in front of the big maps."

"Yeah, but do you understand what they're saying?" asked Rob.

"Who cares? It's the frigging weather."

"Enough with the weather. Is it too early for a beer?" I asked.

"It's never too early when you're on a boat," said Marty, passing out four cold cans of Piels.

"Piels Real Draft? Man, I haven't had one of these in years. Where'd ya get them?" asked Rob.

"The distributor in town. I figured I'd give this stuff a shot again. Brings back memories of my underage drinking days."

Rob took a sip. "Wow, tastes just like beer."

"Thank you, Sam Malone." Marty lifted his drink and continued. "Remember all those local brews we grew up with?"

"What I remember most are the bottles," I replied.

Marty took a long swig. "Yeah, like the chug-a-mugs."

"Or the stubbies," chuckled Rob. "I remember driving back home from college with my trunk full of them because you couldn't buy that beer west of the Mississippi. I got a flat tire on the Jersey Turnpike and an off-duty cop helped me out, so I gave him a six-pack. Thought the guy was gonna kiss me."

"Hell, we used to drink quarts of colt," shouted Steve. "I'm not even sure that was beer."

"It was malt liquor," I said.

"How do you know this stuff?" asked Rob.

"It's gotta be the jellyfish," I joked. "What's everyone up to this weekend? Catey and I promised to help Allie with her yard sale."

"I hear her girls are knock-outs," smirked Rob, wiggling his fingers. "Need an extra set of hands?"

"You pervert. They're your grandkids' age," cried Marty. "And besides, they are way out of your league. Kim, the oldest one, just got into law school at U Penn, my alma mater."

"Wow. That's gotta cost a pretty penny," sighed Steve. "Hopefully, Socket's estate will help Allie out."

"It better because she ain't making squat from the yard sale," I said.

Steve started to laugh.

"Screw you," yelled Rob.

Steve lost it and started laughing harder, and I was doing my best not to crack up more.

"What gives?" asked Marty.

"Okay. Tell him," conceded Rob.

Steve egged me on. "Timbo, you tell the story."

"Okay. About four years ago, Catey and I were at the brewery when this clown showed up with Ginny. I was exhausted because I'd spent the whole day cleaning out the basement and was complaining about the truckload of shit, I had to take to the dump the next morning. Turns out Steve had a lot of crap to throw out too, so I suggested we do a joint run. You know, maybe grab a donut or two afterwards."

"Except," interrupted Steve, "Ginny thought our junk was too good to just toss. She believes that one person's trash is another's treasure. So we had boxes and boxes, with labels on them, stacked in the garage for years because Ginny kept promising to sell or donate the stuff."

"Labeled?" questioned Marty.

"Yeah. A for the very good stuff, B for the good

stuff and C for regular stuff. Don't even ask."

"Anyway," I continued, "I proposed the idea of a yard sale to the wives, but they immediately gave it a thumbs down. So we decided to yard sale someone else—on that very night."

"And they picked me," piped in Rob.

"Well, you were the only sucker, excuse me, person, who came to mind," I said. "So, after a few beers, we went home and started packing up our junk."

"Junk? It was good stuff," said Steve, "the crap we threw away."

"We loaded up our trucks, along with a couple of folding tables and, at midnight, we set everything up on Rob's front lawn. The girls tagged it all, to make it look legit, and even made signs that said *Yard Sale Today 8 a.m. to 4 p.m.*. We had some good stuff: car seats, boogie boards, a towrope for water skiing and some fishing poles. We even put out the shot-ski that I had made with my son Kev."

"You guys are effing nuts," said Marty.

"Wait, wait. It gets better. So the next morning, we rode our bikes to Rob's neighbor's house, getting there a little before eight. There were a bunch of parked cars and a dozen people milling around the place. Finally, at about eight fifteen, a man goes to the front door with one of my old fishing poles and rings the doorbell. We started snickering and acting like ten-year-olds as Sue answered the door in her silk pjs."

"And I'm still in bed," interrupted Rob. "Then I hear Sue downstairs talking to this guy about a yard sale. I look out my window and I see all of this crap on my lawn. So I run downstairs, still in my robe."

"No, it wasn't a robe," corrected Steve. "It was a

vintage, 1960s, Hugh Heffner smoking jacket."

"Whatever," Rob growled. "So I start explaining to the guy that there is no yard sale, when, all of a sudden, Sue flies past me with a glass pitcher in one hand and a mini vac in the other, and yells, 'Oh yes we are. Get dressed! We're definitcly having a yard sale.'"

"I never worked so hard in my life," said Rob. "Those people were animals."

"So did you guys finally go and help him out?" asked Marty.

"We were going to," said Steve, "but the girls were tired, and I was hungry, and Rob looked like he had everything under control."

"Like hell I did," Rob yelped. "I was so sore the next day, I couldn't get out of bed."

"But you made a lot of money, right?" Marty asked.

"A whooping twenty-nine bucks."

Marty turned to me. "And when did you guys fess up? "

"We didn't. The girls ratted us out."

I was still laughing when I felt two hands on my back and suddenly I found myself flying into the bay. I looked up at the boat and saw Rob sitting on the rail howling hysterically.

"Payback's a bitch," he yelled, putting his thumbs in his ears and wiggling his hands.

Just then, Marty and Steve snuck up behind him, grabbed him under his arms, and flipped him into the water. We were all roaring and I thought to myself, "Here we are. Seventy-year old men acting like adolescents. You can't make this stuff up. I'm so fortunate to have these lunatics as my friends."

Without warning, Marty and Steve executed consecutive cannonballs, while Rob shouted, "Did anyone remember to let down the ladder?"

Chapter Twenty

The last time we went out on Steve's boat, the bilge pump started making funny noises. He ordered a new part and planned on replacing it over the weekend. On Saturday, I got a text from him around noon, asking if I had a long-handled, deep-socket ratchet. I searched my toolbox and came up with a few options. I drove over and found him lying on the deck of the boat, his arm immersed in the bilge and his belly protruding from the bottom of his tee shirt. He was sweating like a farm animal. After stepping on board, I heard the distinct sound of a wrench clattering to the ground followed by a loud "Shit!"

"Hey, Steve. Looks like you're having fun."

As he looked up, he bumped his head on the engine "Yeah, I'm having a fucking blast. Can't you tell?"

I couldn't help the grin on my face. "Yep."

"Did you bring that wrench?" he asked, making his way to the cooler and grabbing a cold one.

"I brought this," I said, holding up a foot long, T-handle socket drive.

He downed the beer in three swallows, then crushed the can. "That should work. Changing these pumps should be a simple job," he complained, "but every frigging thing below deck is always a few inches out of reach."

I handed him the wrench, and he got back to work.

A few seconds later, he muttered, "Got it. Finally." He threw the old part on the deck and sat up. "You want a beer?"

"Let's wait till you finish," I replied.

After Steve attached the wires, put the new pump in place, and screwed in the bolts, he yelled, "Hit the switch on the far right there."

I pressed the button and a gurgling sound echoed from the back of the boat, ironically competing with Carole King's *You Got A Friend*.

He got up, secured the hatch, and smiled broadly. "Done, thanks to you, my friend."

"No problem. Everything's easy if you have the right tool. And now I'll have that beer with you." I reached into the cooler and saw two flattened empties. Half-heartedly, I took out a couple of cans and handed one to Steve. "Cheers."

Steve raised his beer but didn't look at me. He just stared out at the water.

"What's wrong, dude?"

"Nothing. Just happy that's over with."

"It's one o'clock and you're on your fourth beer."

"It's hot out here."

"C'mon man, don't bullshit me."

"I'm thirsty."

"Okay."

I grabbed my beer and got up to leave.

"It's Ginny," he said after a moment. "Something's wrong."

"What do you mean?"

"She's not been feeling right. We've been to a bunch of doctors the last few weeks and haven't gotten any definite answers. Finally, she had a PET scan yesterday."

"PET scan, huh? I had a few of them myself. That sucks. They injected me with some dye and my mouth tasted like metal for hours."

He looked away and I could tell that he didn't want to hear about my experience. "We get the results in a few days."

"How's she dealing with all this?"

"Surprisingly, pretty good. Much better than I am; I'm a frigging wreck. We've been together more than fifty years. I don't know what I'd do without her."

"Well, don't jump to conclusions. It could be something simple."

"Cancer is never simple," he said, the words struggling to come out of his mouth.

"Have you told the kids yet?"

"No, nobody. In fact, she'd kill me if she knew I was telling you. You can't tell anyone about this. Not even Catey."

I paused. "I won't."

He stared at me.

"I promise."

We finished our beers and talked about our wives for a while.

"Still up for fishing Monday?"

"We'll see."

Chapter Twenty-One

I drove home, walked into my house and was greeted by a mouthwatering smell coming from the kitchen. "Hey, Cate!"

"Where you been?" she asked.

"Over at Steve's. Helping him replace his bilge pump."

"You fix it?"

"Yep."

She opened the oven, pulled out a rack of chocolate chip cookies and placed them on the counter to cool. Catey was dressed in her summer uniform—no shoes, ratty sweat shorts and one of my old dress shirts. The way she attacked a simple task with determination was one of the qualities I loved most about her. Her graceful movements around the kitchen always brought a smile to my face.

She looked at me. "What?"

"Nothing."

She gave me the look that said, "Get out of here. I'm in the zone."

So I took my wrench, grabbed a cookie, and retreated downstairs. I went to my workbench, started putting things away, but I couldn't concentrate. I kept thinking of Ginny. I couldn't imagine waking up every morning without Catey next to me. The way she laughs at my stupid jokes, the way she interrupts my long stories to tell me she's bored, and even the frustrated look she gives me when I try to help her make the bed are what make her my girl. When I'm sad, she's there, and when the going gets tough, her hands find mine. She's been my planner, my rock and my light for more than forty years. I know I probably sound like a Hallmark card, but it's all true. I'm so friggin' lucky.

Chapter Twenty-Two

Monday morning started out sunny, still, and hot, not at all conducive for landing fish. We made it over to Noyack Bay, dropped our baited hooks, and watched them disappear.

"No movement at all," said Marty after a few minutes, "and we have an hour more of slack tide. How 'bout those damned Yankees? Six home runs and they still lose ten to nine."

"Sue and I have tickets," Rob said.

"To the Yankee game?"

"What game? I'm talking about the musical." Rob placed his hands on his heart and started to sing. "You gotta have…."

"Stop right there," I ordered. "You're scaring the fish."

Rob paid me no mind. He started gyrating in a poor excuse for a belly dance, belting out his next number.

"Hey Marty?" I yelled. "Any tomatoes in that cooler?"

"How about a peach?"

"Beach?" asked Rob. "Allie's girls were there yesterday. In their thongs! He grinned and then segued into another number."

Marty covered his eyes and shook his head. "Please don't tell me you got a boner."

Rob stopped. "Boner," he repeated, thoughtfully. "I

haven't heard that word in a long while. My mom used to use it all the time. Whenever she made a mistake, she would say, 'I pulled a boner.' I thought nothing of it till I turned ten, and then it was embarrassing."

"Speaking of boners, have I got a story for you," I said.

"We have all the time in the world, Timbo," kidded Marty. "We haven't had a nibble yet, and it'll keep this guy from singing."

"It was back in the early eighties when I was a young salesman peddling shipping supplies. I sold markers and packaging tape, but my big item was this new, high-tech machine that printed labels with a 3" x 5" stencil. I carried everything around in this huge, fifty-pound case that had wheels on the bottom like a suitcase. One day I had an important sales demo set up at this large cosmetic company. I even remember the name of the purchasing agent I met with. Tom Jones!"

"With a name like that, it's not unusual," Marty sang. "Heh heh."

"Not you too," I laughed. "So I show up at the main office and introduced myself to this very pretty receptionist, and she tells me, in a British accent, that Tom is in a meeting but could see me in fifteen or twenty minutes. So, I grab a chair, begin daydreaming about the pretty girl behind the desk, and junior starts waking up. Of course, I'm wearing a lightweight suit with boxer shorts underneath, so I have no support."

"I think I know where this is going," cried Marty.

"Yeah, up," said Rob.

"So I reach for a magazine to distract myself and start flipping through the pages, but it's a fashion magazine full of sexy young things, and things start to get worse. Now I'm hard as a rock. All of a sudden, the receptionist gets up, comes over to me and says, 'Mr. Jones will see you now. Follow me.' Now this girl, about twenty-three, was wearing a skirt that should have been illegal. It barely covered her ass. So, I stood up, turned my case sideways, and placed it strategically in front of my crotch. She turns and asks, 'Doesn't that have wheels?' 'Uhh, they're broken,' I stammered, and followed her down the hall. By now, my arm is fucking killing me, and remember, I couldn't rest the case against my body. I thought my arm was going to fall off, but I had to keep that damned thing at least eight inches away because I was still sticking out."

"You're Irish." said Marty. "You could have brought it a lot closer."

"Hey, let Timbo tell his story," chimed Rob.

"Down the hall there was a set of stairs, about nine steps, that she starts to climb. I followed her up with my case still in front of me. Luckily, my woody started to calm down and when we reached the top, she turned around and asked me if I was okay. I said I was fine. She smiled, turned around, wiggled her butt, and I was rock hard all over again. I'm sure she caught on to my awkward condition. I finally got to this guy Tom's office. Luckily, he was on the phone, so he waved me into a chair where I pulled out a few of my catalogs and laid them across my lap."

"Get to the end already," Marty whined. "Did you make the sale?"

"Hold on. So this guy Tom was already sold on the system because he had seen it at a trade show. He just needed to know the price. But he wanted me to demonstrate the machine to the printing department. So he says, 'Let me get Bobby, the print manager, up here.' Well, Bobby just happened to be a five-foot, four-inch brunette in skin-tight jeans and a white tee shirt that showed off all of her good points, if you get what I mean. As soon as she walked in the room, up came Woody. I had to follow her down the stairs to the plant. I started out with my case in front of me again, but after a while, I got tired, Junior got tired, and I just didn't give a damn anymore."

"So did you make the sale, Timbo?" they both asked at the same time.

"Oh yeah! They bought the machine, actually two, and they became my best customer.

After that, I made a point of wearing briefs whenever I visited them."

"But what happened to your boner?" asked Rob.

"That was easy. I was a newlywed, so things happened often and easily back then."

"I remember those days," sighed Rob.

I pulled up my fishing rod. "It looks like my bait is gone and, finally, the water is starting to move."

"Bam! I got one," said Marty. "It feels like a blue or a weakfish. Shit, this sucker is giving me some fight," he yelled, as the line kept spooling off his reel.

"Well you better get it on board soon," said Rob. "I got one, too!"

Marty finally got his catch on the boat, where it measured out at twenty-six inches. It was, indeed, a beautiful weakfish. Rob's was smaller, about nineteen, but still a good-size keeper.

Weaks are the prettiest fish in our waters, long and lean with classic streamlined fins and skin speckled with green and purple metallic tints. Tasty too.

Although you can't toss them directly on a grill, but when wrapped in tin foil and sautéed in butter, um, um, scrumptious.

"Nice fish, guys, but remember, the limit on these is one per man," said Marty.

"Speaking of remembering, how's it going with those jellyfish?" I asked.

"Working for me," said Rob. "I was playing a matching game with the grandkids last week, whipping their tails, till Sue started kicking me under the table."

"How about you, Marty?" I asked. "Still making you horny?"

"Everything makes me horny. Hey, last night I got the final Jeopardy question right."

"I missed it yesterday. What was it?"

"Who was the first silent film star to sign a million-dollar contract?"

"Buster Keaton?"

"Close, but no cigar," he said, in his best Groucho impersonation. "Charlie Chaplin."

Rob and I laughed, while Steve sat silent munching on a caramel.

Chapter Twenty-Three

The following weekend, Marty and I paddled over to Southold Bay for some clamming. Clams come in a variety of sizes, the smallest being the littlenecks. They're about two inches in diameter and best served raw on the half shell with a squirt of lemon, cocktail sauce and sometimes a drop of tequila. Cherrystones are a little bigger, a bit tougher, and taste great when steamed with butter, garlic and white wine. Chowder clams, the largest, are usually baked or reserved for soup and sauce.

When we met up with Rob, he was already standing in a foot of water, pulling his clam rake back and forth. He caught his mollusks the old-fashioned way, straining his back to scrape the surface of the sand, but I preferred sitting in my kayak using my hands to dig them up. I was happy to see Steve out and about, sitting on the bow of Rob's nineteen-footer. I could only imagine the kind of hell he was going through.

"Looks like a lot of work for a few clams," said Marty.

"That's what I told him," Steve agreed.

"You know, Charlie's fish market sells them for five dollars a dozen," I said.

"Yeah, but that's for the chowder clams," said Rob. "I'm looking for smaller ones. And besides, this is so much more fun."

"Yeah, looks like a blast," cracked Steve, "sweating your ass off in the hot sun to save a nickel."

Every time I saw someone clamming, it brought me back to that morning years ago by Flower Beach. Sinatra sang about a few regrets, while living life his way. Well, I've got one big one that still bothers me. If only I had stopped that day.

We continued to razz Rob for a while when Marty announced, "Here come the law."

In minutes, a small patrol boat pulled up beside us. A guy hopped off the boat, wearing shorts and a gray tee shirt emblazoned with Southold Police Department. It was Joe Wizkowski.

"Well, if it isn't Officer Wiz," I announced sarcastically.

"You guys have a license for clamming here?"

"What's it to you?" snapped Marty.

"Well, if you haven't heard yet, I am now an employee of the town," he said, proudly pointing to his shirt.

"No shit! They took you back?" I asked, incredulous.

"What's it to you?" he snapped right back. "License?"

"It's in my wallet," yelled Rob, "on the boat."

"And we're not clamming," clarified Marty. "We're just here to hassle him."

To our surprise, Officer Wiz cracked a smile. "And I'm just busting your chops. I only wanted to thank you guys for helping out Allie."

"No problem. She's good people," I said, and wished him good luck on the job.

As soon as he was out of earshot, I heard Marty say, "What a jackass." Then he turned to us. "Anyone besides me have problems with the fuzz growing up?"

"I did," said Rob. "When I was a kid, there was this Irish cop named Flanagan who walked the beat in my neighborhood. He ruled the Bronx with his nightstick and, never fail, he loved to rap me on the shins whenever he saw me, even if I was doing nothing. And, man, it hurt like hell."

"Yeah, the cops were always busting on me, too," said Marty. "When I was about twelve, I used to hang out with these older guys who were doing things like hot-wiring cars and stealing hubcaps. The police were always hassling me, and, once, they even patted me down and took away my switchblade. My stepbrother was a city cop, and I think it was his screwed-up way of looking out for me."

"I have a story, too," I said.

"Please Timbo. Not another one of your long-winded epics," said Steve.

I ignored him and continued. "Well, it was during Easter vacation. I was about eleven, messing around at my friend Billy's house, and we decided to go to the Gold Arches for lunch. Now the closest one was on Hempstead Turnpike, about four miles away and two towns over. We decided to ride Billy's brand-new bike, a neon blue stingray, with oversized handlebars and a banana seat that fit two."

"Here we go again with the damn details," complained Steve, pulling a peanut cluster out of his pocket.

Knowing his mind was probably somewhere else, I took no offense and carried on. "So, after we finished our fries, we headed home, taking the bicycle path along the parkway. On our way, we stopped at this overpass and started spitting over the side at the cars driving below. There was hardly any traffic in the middle of the day, so our chance of hitting a car with our spittle was nearly impossible."

"I hope this gets better," complained Marty.

"So, I worked up this really big phlegm that was thick like syrup, and real gooey, and I leaned my head over the rail and launched this vile clam downward. It started out elastic, like a drool, and was probably about six inches long when it finally left my lips. From a distance, I could see a big black Plymouth approaching, and bingo! My drool touched down smack in the middle of the windshield."

"Now, this is getting interesting," said Marty.

"Suddenly, I hear tires skidding, brakes screeching, and Billy screaming, 'Oh shit! Run! The guy is coming after us!' Well, we didn't get very far. The loudest voice I'd ever heard in my life shouted 'Stop!' Billy and I froze in our tracks. The man getting out of the car was the tallest, meanest-looking policeman I had ever seen. He was hatless and wore a crisp blue uniform, but all I noticed was his bright gold shield and his gun. 'Stop right there,' he ordered. 'Which one of you juvenile delinquents is responsible for this disgusting slobber?' Before I could say anything, I noticed Billy's finger pointing in my direction, and I knew it was time to spill. And so I did. 'Get over here and clean this mess up!" yelled the cop. So, I reached into the left pocket of my dungarees, but all I found was loose change. From the right one, I pulled out my Cub Scout pocketknife, then a pack of matches, and last, the napkin from my burger meal. I ran over to the car, cleaned up the gunk, and turned to leave. 'Not so fast. I need names and addresses,' said the copper, and, way too quickly I gave mine up. Billy the street-smart kid, on the other hand, made up a phony ID. After the cop drove away, Billy said, 'You're a jerk. Why'd you give him your real address? Don't you know what's coming in the mail?' I had no clue, but Billy explained that a JD card was on its way. All that week I was shittin' in my pants. And on Monday, when I got home from school, my mom's all pissed because I was late. When I heard, 'Timothy, get in here," I knew I was screwed. Except I wasn't. Turns out I had forgotten about my dentist appointment. Go figure, sometimes you just get lucky."

"So after all that spit you went through, you never got you badge of dishonor?" joked Marty.

"Nope! No more run-ins for a few more years. But those are stories for some other day."

"Thank God," said Steve, looking at his phone, but I wasn't quite sure what he meant.

Chapter Twenty-Four

Officer Wiz's first day back on the force was uneventful. At noon, he reported to headquarters for a brief meeting with Chief Barkley, who gave him his first assignment patrolling a music event. He was partnered with a rookie named Justin.

The Blues Festival was held at a local winery. The first band would start at two o'clock; the final act was scheduled for six. Their instructions were to direct traffic, keep the crowd under control, and to search all coolers for liquor and beer. The preconcert sounds, about fifteen minutes of amplified, scratchy music, had the crowd restless on this warm summer afternoon until a solo guitarist took the stage and silenced the riff-raff with a B. B. King classic. The audience got into it, swaying and singing along, and the two cops headed for some shade.

"Hey Joe," said Justin. "Haven't I seen you before? At the gym maybe? Shooting hoops?"

"Yeah. I still go there once in a while. I was on the high school team with Ed, I mean Chief Barkley."

"Shit, you played with the Chief?"

"Yeah. He was the point guard and I played forward. Brains and Brawn, they called us. League champs our senior year.

Between the first and second acts, two jerks were trying to set up a big canopy in the center of the field, blocking the view of half the concertgoers. Joe and Justin headed over and told the fellas to put it away or move it to the back row. Satisfied there was no flack, they grabbed lunch and sat listening to a young generation of bluesmen playing the tunes of Muddy Waters and John Lee Hooker.

At the table, Joe asked his new partner, "You from around here?"

"Mattituck."

"My ex was from there. Met her at the Strawberry Festival; she led the parade."

"Your wife was the strawberry queen?"

"Runner up."

"If you don't mind my asking, what happened?"

"The usual. Got married young, had a kid right away. She didn't like my friends. I didn't like hers."

As the day wore on, the faint smell of marijuana permeated the air, but there were no incidents that required anything more than a serious leer or a stern word of advice. The final act was a young, sexy, sparkplug named Sage, who couldn't be older than twenty. The crowd went crazy when she started belting out numbers made famous by Janis Joplin, Billie Holliday and Bonnie Raitt. By night's end, there must have been thirty musicians up on the stage jamming.

When their first shift was over, Justin shook Joe's hand, and welcomed him back on the job. And when they hit the locker room, the veteran got a standing O from his old buddies "Heeeeere's Joey," they cheered as he entered their sanctuary.

Then all the guys started singing that Gene Autry ditty about riding your horse, toting a gun and being back on the job.

All smiles, Joe hugged his cronies, then started changing as they peppered him with questions.

"So how was your first day?"

"Good, but hotter than I remember."

"Any hot babes at that winery, Joe?"

He just laughed.

"I hear you've been hanging out with somebody's granddaughter. Trying to rob the cradle?"

"Screw you," Joe smiled, keeping it light.

"It's good to have you back, buddy. Come grab a beer with us."

"Thanks, but I'll take a rain check," he begged off, pointing to his toes. "These feet of mine need some rest. They're used to sneakers and flip flops."

Everyone laughed.

Joe had the following day off. He felt happy but, at the same time, lonely. He thought about visiting Allie but quickly nixed the idea. Why spend four hours in a car driving to see someone when he really wasn't that into her. And besides, she knew nothing about Socket's stash.

Chapter Twenty-Five

Next morning Marty was sitting on his dock untangling lines when I said I was going for a ride. "I'm in," he said. "Just let me get my pole. Steve coming?"

"Nah, he can't make it."

"Just as well."

I wasn't gonna go there, so I ignored his comment. "Let's check out Clam Island."

Clam Island is a small speck on the South Fork at the base of Jessup's Neck. The narrow passage that divides the island from the mainland is the only access to picturesque Noyack Creek and is off limits to bathers.

"Sounds good," said Marty. "Isn't that where the Hampton chicks sunbathe? Nude? If we don't catch fish, maybe we can catch an eyeful."

I gave him a thumbs-up. We took our time puttering over to our spot, rigged up our poles with diamond jigs, and drifted east in search of bluefish, or something.

"Nothing biting here," I moaned after a while.

"But there's our shadow again," he said, nodding his head.

I looked over and saw the Wiz in his cat boat. "He doesn't give up, does he?"

"He probably wants the pot more that we do."

Sure enough, the other boat was keeping a sharp

watch on our progress. We worked our way through the shallow channel, and we decided to give it another shot.

"What's in this creek, anyway?" asked Marty.

"Flounder, I hope."

"I haven't caught one of those in years," he said.

"Me neither. As kids, we called them black-backs or fatties because of their dark coloring and thickness. I only found out a few years ago how to tell a flounder from a fluke. If you lay them flat on the deck, the eyes of a fluke face left and the flounder's look right."

"Yeah, and fluke are much bigger," added Marty. "Minimum size for flounder is twelve inches and fluke is nineteen. Best bait for them is a bloodworm, but they'll eat anything when they're hungry."

"Bloodworms! Those things are nasty," I said. "Did you ever get bit by one?"

"Didn't everybody? Those four prongs would come out of their mouths, like the monster in *Alien,* and latch themselves on the tip of your finger. It hurt like hell!"

I put a small hook on my rig, baited it with a clam strip, and tossed it in the water.

"Look who's coming to join us," chuckled Marty.

"I'm surprised he made it through that two-foot inlet with those double Vs."

"Double Ds? Where?" Marty whooped, looking around for the closest babe.

"Is that all you think about?"

He laughed. "Blame it on the jellyfish."

"Yeah. Right."

"Screw you. Let's just get out of here while we can."

"Yeah, but before we go," I proposed, "what do

you say we mess with the Wiz a little?"

I took off my shirt, dove in the water, and swam to shore. I walked around a bit, rustled some tall bushes, and dug up a few weeds. Back on the boat, I ceremoniously handed Marty the greens. "This is what you call setting the hook."

He burst out laughing. "Someone's gonna be late for lunch, and it ain't gonna be us."

Chapter Twenty-Six

As a senior in high school, Joe Wizkowski went halves on a small speedboat with one of his pals. They spent their vacation cruising the bays, water-skiing, and racing against friends. Then the engine crapped out and that was that.

The following fall, Joe was hired as a cadet in the Southold Police Department and life took over. He never got the chance to own another boat, but today he was basking in the luxury of a twenty-four-footer. Joe was keeping an eye on Dr. Thomas Cook's properties while the surgeon was playing in Paris with his new girlfriend.

Wiz was on a mission. He knew that Socket had a pot farm somewhere in the area and he was banking on Tim and his buddies to lead him there. This morning he was hot on their tail, just waiting for one of them to tip his hand. All Wiz needed was one measly plant, a nice chunk of change, his old job back on the force, and he'd be set for life. He could finally move out of his mom's condo, maybe buy a small house in town, or look for a place in Florida.

Bored out of his gourd, Joe sat for over an hour watching the two pals fish, when all of a sudden things started to get interesting. One of them jumped into the water and swam to the beach. But by the time Joe started the engine, the swimmer was already back on board, and it looked like he was waving something up in the air.

Joe grinned. "Holy shit."

He couldn't wait for those clowns to be gone so he could go exploring. Once they were out of sight, the private eye found the tracks in the sand easy enough and headed into the woods searching for the Holy Grail. He spotted some tall grasses and eagerly marched in their direction. Nothing but phragmites, bushes, and poison ivy. Totally disgusted, Wiz walked back to his boat and started for home. He had a two o'clock appointment with Chief Barkley that he didn't want to miss. As Joe approached the inlet, he noticed that the water had receded considerably, but he steered his craft into the channel anyway. Then, all movement came to a halt. He glanced over the side and could see the bottom clearly.

"Damn it!" He lifted the engine, jumped into the mud, and started pushing the boat. "I'm fucking stuck," he cried out to no one.

Wading to the front and pushing with all his might didn't help. "Damn it!" he yelled again, climbing back on. Realizing he'd be here all afternoon, he kicked the console and swatted at a green fly. "Shit, shit, shit!"

It suddenly occurred to Joe just how alone he was. He took out his phone, left a message for the Chief, and lay down on the cushions. He closed his eyes to stop the tears.

Chapter Twenty-Seven

After lounging around all morning, I took my paddleboard out for a spin. It was my happy place. As the blade sliced the water, I started thinking about Officer Wiz. Why did I dislike him? It had nothing to do with his job. Some of my best friends were cops. Ha ha. But there was something about him that always rubbed me the wrong way. Whenever I saw Joe, he was always alone. No wife, no girlfriend—that I knew of— and a kid a thousand miles away.

Catey calls him a lost soul and maybe he is. He never seems totally comfortable around people, especially those he doesn't know. And with a couple of beers in his belly, he turns into a real dufus, always saying the wrong thing at the wrong time. Trying desperately to be cool, desperately to belong, but always ending up on the outside of the in crowd. Maybe I just feel sorry for him; seems like he's trying too hard to be something he's not, like a badass cop. And though most of the time he irks the hell out of me, I bet deep down he's a good egg.

A large wake came by and shook my board. Instinctively, I shifted my weight to keep my balance and saw two large crabs scoot by, followed by three smaller blue claws. Perhaps they're on their way to a crayfish reunion, I mused.

Family and friends. Maybe that's what's missing in

Joe's life. I know I'd be lost without mine. Catey, Kevin and all those guys who keep me honest. Fishing buddies, softball guys, golf geeks. Heck, I still have friends from grammar school. I know I could trust any one of these guys with my life. Through all the beers and BS, we've always had one another's back.

I heard someone yelling from the shore and looked to see Catey standing in the water watching our dog swim out to greet me. When Callahan's two paws landed on the front of my board, I knew I was in trouble. All of a sudden, I was floundering in the creek, trying to hold on to my board. I came up, wiped the water from my eyes, and opened my arms to Catey, who was laughing hysterically.

Chapter Twenty-Eight

Officer Wiz was sleeping on the bow when his cell phone rang. It was the chief. "Hello?"

"I got your message. Where are you? It sounds like you're half asleep."

"No sir. I'm over here at the County Center. My ex and I had some legal issues to resolve, and things got delayed. Is it possible to meet a little later today?"

Ed Barkley shook his head. He had been married to Peg, the love of his life, for over twenty-five years and still relished his weekends. He could take off his uniform, be a husband, and play dad to his two daughters. He never understood why Joe screwed around on his wife. Growing up, Ed and Joe were pals. In grammar school they were inseparable, but things changed when they got to high school. On the court, they were the dynamic duo, but that's where it ended, and after graduation, Ed went to college and Joe joined the force.

"How's six o'clock, Joe?"

"Perfect. Thanks."

"But do me a favor."

"Sure, boss. Anything."

"On the way home, stop by the courthouse and pick up an arraignment file. I'll call the receptionist and tell her you're coming."

Joe hung up, glanced at his watch, and yelled at the

top of his lungs. "Joseph Wizkowski, you are one dumb jackass. It's already two-fifteen. Even if you get out of this fucking creek by four, it's gonna be tight. You need to bring back the boat, drive home, go back to Riverhead, and be at the police building by six. Why do you always get yourself into these fucked up situations?"

Frustrated, he punched the windshield with his fist. He bemoaned his bad luck, envious that Ed fast-tracked to detective while poor, working-class Joe was still ticketing jaywalkers and chasing DWIs. He had so many regrets. His marriage to Sally. His divorce from Sally. His fling with Donna. His break-up with Donna. And worst of all, a son who didn't really like him. Joe reached for his flask and took a healthy swig.

****

Miraculously, at six o'clock sharp, Wiz pulled into the parking lot, file in hand. He tapped on the office door and the Chief waved him in. "Take a seat, Joe. Just give me a few minutes." When Barkley finally got off the phone, he got up to stretch. "If I knew how much paperwork was involved, I never would have taken this job. I really miss the action."

"I know what you mean, sir."

"Here's what I wanted to talk to you about. Taxpayers are complaining about the increase of incidents in the bays. The usual stuff—excessive speeding, boating while under the influence, and litter on our beaches. Unfortunately, right now, we have only two boats, the twenty-foot scout and the twenty-seven-foot cruiser. I was thinking that with five extra shifts a week, we could make a significant difference. Any interest?"

"Yes sir, I'd like that very much."

"I thought so," Barkley smiled. "Truthfully, I thought you were given a raw deal back then. Circumstances were way beyond your control."

"Thanks Ed, I mean, Chief."

"You don't have to be so formal with an old friend, Joe."

"Appreciate that, Ed."

"So here's the scoop. Word has it illegal immigrants are coming by boat to the East End, where they can work as cooks or maids, especially in the Hamptons. Your new assignment requires some long days, but I think it's a good path towards reinstatement."

"I really appreciate this. You free for a beer? My treat."

"Some other time. Peg's got dinner waiting for me at home. And, Joe, one more thing. You should really start wearing sunscreen. That's quite a burn you got."

Joe drove home to an empty condo. He showered, changed, and splashed on some aftershave.

He walked down to Founders and sat at the corner of the near-empty bar. Lucy, the bartender, stared at him with none too friendly eyes as she handed him a double shot of vodka on the rocks. "Want a burger with that?"

"Sure. Thanks."

She brought him his food, poured him another round, and left him alone to soak up the tension. She wasn't in the mood tonight for another Officer Wiz shit show. Lucy had many hours of inventory ahead of her and no patience for his nonsense. She pulled out a stool to grab something off the top shelf when Joe unexpectedly stood.

"Let me get that for you."

"And they say chivalry is dead." She gave him a look, then grinned. "Thank you, officer."

"How'd you know about that?"

"Small town. One bar. I hear it all."

Joe laughed and then so did she. It was dark out by the time Joe left the pub, and as he passed the Historical Society, his son called. Joe couldn't answer fast enough. "Hey, Ryan."

"Hey, Dad. You rang?"

"Yeah, was just checking in to see how you're doing."

"All good."

"I hear it's hot as hell in Florida these days."

"Yeah. What's up?"

"Good news; I started working for the department again."

"Wow. How'd that happen?"

For the next twenty minutes they talked shop. Finally, father and son were finding their way back. After he hung up, Joe cautioned himself. "You better not screw this up."

Chapter Twenty-Nine

Wednesday morning, we all met at Marty's house for our excursion to the pizza place in Connecticut. In the driveway, I turned to Steve. "How's Ginny doing? Any news?"

"Nothing yet," he whispered, hopping in to a brand new, electric SUV. Though we had plenty of time before our 10:00 a.m. ferry, Marty showed off his car's dynamic acceleration, going from zero to sixty, in three seconds. The G force repelled us to our seat backs, and our stomachs turned as adrenaline exploded in our mouths.

"Do that again," Rob threatened, "and my breakfast will be decorating your ponytail."

We all laughed as we hit the road singing Willie Nelson's anthem. Marty parked on the lower deck of the ferry and we went upstairs to a window table, ordered coffee, and listened to the foghorn.

The Cross Sound Ferry has been in existence more than a hundred years, shuttling people and cars from Orient Point to New London. Our launch, *The Cape Hennepin*, was built in 1943 and once served as a landing craft for American troops on D-Day. The trip took about an hour and a half, still the shortest way to get from the North Fork to Providence and Boston. At the very end of the island stood a lighthouse nicknamed the Coffee Pot, which guarded the dangerous waters of

Plum Gut. The currents that race though this narrow inlet connecting the Sound with Gardiners Bay, can reach five or more knots. Add a strong wind and the water can be treacherous. Today, the conditions were calm.

"They're quite a few fishing boats in the Gut," I observed.

"Charter boats looking for stripers," explained Marty.

"Slim pickings this time of year," stated Steve. "It looks like they're trolling."

"Trolling on a charter boat sucks," I noted. "You're constantly moving, the mate is handling the fishing rods, whipping them up and down, and then, when you finally get a hit, he hands you the pole to reel in the fish. It's like playing golf and having your caddy carry your bag, hit all your shots, then hand you the putter when you're on the green."

"Well, I wouldn't go that far," said Marty. "But I agree that the best part of fishing is the strike, especially when it's a striper."

Striped bass— stripers—are beautiful fish: silvery gray in color with a long, streamlined body, forked tail, and seven or eight narrow, horizontal stripes adorning their sides. These are the primo game fish on Long Island, home of record catches of up to fifty inches and over sixty pounds. Interestingly enough, they have no teeth, just gums, rough like sandpaper, allowing them to devour their prey. The big ones thrive in this deep water.

"I've lost more sinkers and rigs down there than I can count," said Steve. "The bottom of Plum Gut must be paved in lead."

"I've never had much luck here," sighed Rob.

"You gotta fish at night with eels," informed Marty, "but it's one long ride home in the dark."

"Look at that boat," said Rob, pointing to a small, twelve-foot aluminum dinghy with two kids on board. "How old do you think they are? Ten? Twelve? If a rogue wave came along, they would capsize in a minute. Dopey kids."

I made a face. "Right, like you didn't do stupid stuff when you were a kid?"

"Sure, but nothing that could have killed me."

"What?" I aimed my trigger finger at him. "You never smoked the barrel of your cap gun?"

Rob stared at me as Steve and Marty started to giggle. "I never heard of that. What do you mean?"

"Didn't you have a cap pistol when you were a kid?" I asked him.

"Sure, but . . . . ."

"When you finished shooting a roll of caps, smoke would come out of the barrel. Cool kids, like me, would put the gun under their mouths and inhale the smoke."

Everyone cracked up.

"How about testing a 9 volt battery?" asked Steve, sticking out his tongue.

"I remember that," said Marty. "My buddy got me good with it. We were listening to his transistor radio when it went dead. So he pulls a new copper-top out of his pocket and asks me to test it. And dumb ass me put the thing on my tongue and, boy, did I get the shock of my life."

"My brother once got me good with the lawnmower spark plug," I said. "He asked me to hold the wire, so like an idiot, I did, and then he pulls the recoil and electricity starts flowing through my arm till it's numb. And he's just watching, laughing his ass off."

We talked about mindless crap like this for a while until, suddenly, the USS Delaware, a Virginia class submarine, broke the water's surface right there in front of our eyes.

"Wow. That's some ship," remarked Steve. "I wonder if they're out on maneuvers from the base."

"You think they're looking for Socket's pot, too?" asked Rob.

I started choking on my coffee.

The ferry docked, and, an hour later, we were in the crowded parking lot of an old building. At the front door was a wooden sign in the shape of a man, wearing a chef's hat and holding a big pie that read *Via Pizza*. Inside, a long line of customers waited for take-out, but the dining room was only half-full. Empty Chianti bottles filled with fake flowers rested on red and white-checkered tablecloths.

"Hey, Martino," I called, talking with my hands. "They gotta you favorite Italian beer on tappa,"

Marty grabbed my arm, kissed my pinky, and headed to a nearby booth, where Rob and Steve were already perusing the menu. "Bless you, my son. Is one pie enough?"

"For starters," Steve shouted.

A few minutes later, just as I was getting comfortable, a dark-haired beauty approached carrying a tray with four tall glasses. "Hi, my name is Julie and I'll be your server today."

"Can't wait to taste the pizza; this is our first time here," said Marty. "Has this place been around for a while?"

"Almost fifty years," she said. "Be right back with your food."

"I like this joint," said Steve. "Great atmosphere, feels like Little Italy in the sixties."

"Yeah, but the music is way better here," said Rob. "I'll take Buffalo Springfield over opera any day."

"Julie's not too shabby either," said Marty, as she came towards us with our pie and four plates.

"Four more?" she asked, glancing at our half-full glasses.

"*Grazie*," I said and nodded. "Hey, is there any way we can speak to the owner?"

"He's in the back cooking, but I'll check and see if he can stop by."

As she strolled away, we each grabbed a slice. Steve dug in and his eyes lit up. "This is beyond amazing," he said, and almost drooled. "The crust is thin and crispy, the cheese is bubbling, and the sauce is perfectly spiced."

"You mind posting that on Yelp?" asked a middle-aged man in jeans and a flour-dusted apron. "Hi, I'm Sal, the owner. Julie said that you wanted to see me?"

I put down my food. "A friend of ours passed away recently and we were wondering if you knew him. We found your number stashed away in a book and we think it might be important."

"Perhaps he was ordering take out?" Sal offered.

"No," I continued. "We're not from around here. We live on Long Island."

"And you guys came all the way to Connecticut?" He shook his head. "What's your friend's name?"

"John Toomey."

"Sorry, doesn't ring a bell. How old was he?"

"Mid-seventies."

"You might wanna talk to my dad; he owned the place before me."

"He around?"

"He's right there in the back. "

At the far end of the store, alone in the corner booth, sat a heavyset man with gray hair and a black Yankee cap. "Hey, Pops," yelled Sal. "These guys wanna talk to you."

I stood and so did Marty who signaled the others to stay put. "We don't want to overwhelm the poor guy."

"I'm gonna grab a couple more slices," said Steve. "Best pizza I've had in years."

Sal smiled. "Watch out for my old man," he warned. "Once you get him started, he doesn't shut up."

As Marty and I walked over to his table, the old guy eyed us suspiciously. "I'm Aldo; what can I do for you?"

"Great place you got here," I started. "Best pizza I've had in years. Came over on the ferry this morning. We're hoping you can do us a favor."

Aldo opened his hand in an 'ask me' motion.

"A friend of ours died recently and we found your phone number on his notepad."

"Your friend was probably ordering pizza."

"That's what your son said," laughed Marty. "But no way we could keep a pie warm all the way back to Long Island."

The old man chuckled. "What was your friend's name?"

"John Toomey, but we always called him Socket," I said.

"I'm not that great with names anymore."

"He was a Vietnam vet, lived off the land, fishing, farming, clamming," I added.

"You mean Skinny John?" Aldo got very excited, as he pulled a grainy photo of two young men in uniform from his wallet. "Is this the guy?"

"Yeah, that's him," we cried.

"We used to call him Skinny John over there. He was lean and lanky, only weighed a buck and a half soakin' wet. I met him on the bus to basic; we served together in the same patrol." Aldo took a deep breath. "Please, have a seat. What happened to John?"

"We found him on his fishing boat passed out. He hit his head on the console. We think he had a stroke."

"I haven't seen him in almost twenty years. One time, he came across the Sound in this little boat, joking that he was in the mood for pizza. Back in the eighties, we marched in that ticker tape parade on Wall Street. Got drunk as skunks that night, twelve of us flopped on the floor of a room at The Diplomat Hotel. Drunk and high! Skinny John always had good weed. He walked the whole distance, even with his bum wheel."

"How did he hurt his leg anyway?" Marty wanted to know.

"Out on patrol. We were in this tiny village, outside of Tan An, north of Ho Chi Min City by the Cambodian border. Skinny John was tossing a baseball around with these three local kids. He had a baseball mitt with him all the time. Was a pitcher back in high school. After he got out, he wanted to go to college and play ball. Even dreamed of turning pro; he could really put a spin on the ball." Aldo took a sip of water. "Anyway, he was talking to these three kids, I think they were brothers, and Skinny—did I tell you that we called him just Skinny sometimes—well, he had a crush on their older sister. So John and these kids are on the edge of a clearing and he's teaching them how to throw the curveball. He did this all the time, and he could really put a spin on the ball. He'd place the ball into their hands, adjusting their fingers till the ball felt just so. They were laughing and smiling; he was a happy guy and loved the kids over there. All of a sudden, from the woods comes a homemade grenade and it lands right next to them. Skinny pushes the boys away and dives on top of them. There's a big explosion and when the shit clears, the three kids get up but Skinny doesn't. A piece of shrapnel is sticking out of his upper leg by his hamstring and his whole back is covered in blood."

Aldo stopped talking and just stared into space. Everything was quiet for a moment. We were between songs, but then a drumroll signaled the start of a Rolling Stones classic, and he smiled. "This is one of my favorite songs. You know, Skinny helped me set up the music when I opened this place years ago. I wanted a jukebox, but he talked me into making tapes of the songs that we grew up with, sixties and early seventies only—Beatles, the Doors, Motown, the Stones, even some Doo-wop stuff. Everyone who comes into my place always compliments me on the music, so why mess with success?"

"So what happened to John?" prodded Marty.

"The medics picked him up, sent him to the hospital, and he got a free ride home. I got back a few months later and we kept in touch for years. Sometimes, he would take his boat across the Sound to see me. And did I tell you guys that once he came all the way over here just for a slice? Ate it and went home. And did you know that he worked in a nursery for a while? And then he did some commercial fishing and clamming. Never got married. I think the accident did some damage to his balls, but he never spoke about it."

Aldo stared into space again, then took a napkin from the dispenser to wipe his eyes. A Jerry Lee Lewis-like musical riff came over the speakers and a distinctive voice started singing a simple tune. "Hey, this was Skinny's favorite song. I have songs for all the guys in my patrol, just upbeat stuff. No protest songs or depressing melodies. We left all that shit behind us in 'Nam."

Sal came over to the table. "Com'on Pops. We gotta go."

"That's right," gloated Aldo. "I'm going to see my grandson play ball. He's pitching. I tried to teach him the curveball grip that I learned from Skinny, but Sal won't let the kid throw it."

"He's too young," Sal said "I don't want him blowing out his shoulder at twelve. He needs to build up his arm strength."

We said our goodbyes and went back to our table.

"What d'ya learn? asked Rob.

"Not much. Probably a dead end, but we did learn Socket's favorite song," I said. "They just played it. That one by the Chuck Berry wannabe."

"That was Dee Clark. Early sixties," clarified Rob. Off key, he started singing about this little girl wearing a high school sweater, chewing gum and looking like a luscious plum.

I laughed. "Those jellyfish sure are working."

Rob looked at me but said nothing.

"Maybe for his memory, but definitely not for his voice," chimed Steve.

Just then a loud clap of thunder blasted through the speakers as The Ronettes started harmonizing about strolling in a storm.

"Wow. I can't believe the music in this place. The sound system is first rate and the song selections are incredible," said Rob, his head bopping.

"Yeah. Ronnie Spector's voice can make anything romantic. Even the rain," I agreed.

I signaled for the check, but Julie waved us off. "Lunch is on Nonno."

Marty and I reached into our pockets and threw a couple of twenties on the table. Steve followed suit. Rob retrieved his massive wallet from his back pocket, put a ten on the table, hesitated, then took out two more.

We walked out, got into the car, and headed back to the ferry. Marty turned on his fancy, schmancy sound system. "What do you guys want? CCR? Doors?"

"No, Zappa," yelled Rob. "Socket was really into him."

Marty slowly said "Zap-pa," out loud, and all of a sudden the speakers erupted with the twang of an eighties California Val-speak accent.

"That's not Frank Zappa," said Rob. "It's his daughter Sunshine, no, Moon."

"Frank Zap-pa," enunciated Marty, and a verse about sled dogs in the Artic came on.

"No, not that one," said Rob. "Damn, I can't remember the name of the song that Socket liked."

"Wait a minute. Did you stop taking your jellyfish?" asked Marty.

Rob was silent.

"You really stopped?" I asked.

"I had to," he answered. "I didn't like the side effects."

"Side effects? What side effects?" fretted Steve.

"Well, you know, down there." Rob looked at his crotch.

"What the hell. You're eighty years old. It ain't gonna work like when you were sixteen."

"Hey, I'm only seventy-five. And, I'm trying to concentrate here. I think it was something about Dinah or Dynamite."

"Someone's in the kitchen with Dinah," I spouted. "Isn't that from I've been working on the railroad."

"Yep," said Marty. "And so is Dinah won't you blow my horn. Pretty racy lyrics for the old days."

"Hey, they were railroad workers, what'd you expect?" I asked.

"I can't believe that nobody else remembers," yelled Rob. "You know, the song about the girl who couldn't get off. Guy spends three hours rubbing her and he still couldn't get her excited."

"That's right," I recalled. "And her sister was naked too. It was like an audio orgy. No wonder it was Socket's favorite song,"

Marty spoke to the stereo. "Play Frank Zap-pa's Dy-na-mite some-thing."

Nothing happened.

"*Dinah-Moe-Humm*," shouted an elated Rob from the back seat, and the sound of bongo drums came on the speakers. A melodic voice started singing about a girl and a guy trying to have sex and her sister wagering that she couldn't. And there was a sexy female voice in the background. The song continued for five more grueling minutes, but the four of us enjoyed every salacious moment of the X-rated lyrics.

"I don't think Cousin Brucie ever played that one," I said when it was finally over.

"Pretty bizarre stuff," said Steve.

Rob seemed puzzled. "I wonder why all these song writers refer to female body parts as fruit. You know peaches, plums, cherries."

"You're as weird as Zappa," said Marty, driving on to the ferry ramp. After parking the car, we bee-lined it to the bar for beers then headed up to the sun deck. It was warm, but soon enough we were rewarded with a cool breeze.

There was always an interesting mix of passengers on board. Vacationers from New England, businessmen returning home, and gamblers from the Connecticut casinos. A group of young men sat opposite us, smoking cigars and drinking booze and talking about last night's adventure in a Rhode Island gentlemen's club. One guy, wearing a glittery tee shirt, was trying to balance a bunch of brews. He nearly wiped out on a slippery spot, but Rob grabbed him just in time.

"Looks like Tinker Bell is sloshed," chuckled Marty. "And what's with the fairy dust?"

I started laughing. "It's stripper glitter. All the dancers wear it. If you get close to them, the stuff magically sticks on to your skin and clothes. And you can't get that shit off. You can wash your face and hands for hours with no luck. Those sparkles have caught more guys than the FBI," I laughed.

"You sound like you're talking from experience," cracked Marty.

"It was a long time ago and a galaxy far, far away."

Steve leaned back and closed his eyes. I wondered if he was dreading going home or just savoring the moment.

We drove off the ferry and Marty put on the stereo; by chance that Dee Clark tune came on again. "That's it," I shouted.

"What?" asked Rob.

"Plum! Sugar plum! Juicy plum! That's what Socket was trying to tell us."

"Plum?" Steve looked dazed.

"Plum Island!" I emphasized.

Marty excitedly pounded the steering wheel. "Plum Island, of course. Why didn't I think of that before?"

Chapter Thirty

Plum Island is a small speck of land situated in Gardiners Bay east of Orient Point. It measures three miles long and one mile wide, but the eastern third is only a few hundred yards across. The island is the site of Plum Island Animal Disease Center; it's owned by the federal government and controlled by the United States Department of Homeland Security. Because of the mysterious ongoing research at the lab, the land is restricted and heavily guarded by federal agents.

"Do you really think Socket's farm could be there?" I wondered out loud as we drove along Gardiners Bay.

"Only one way to find out," said Marty.

"Could be dangerous," piped Steve.

"Yeah," agreed Rob. "I knew a guy who had engine trouble over there and beached his boat on the sandy side of Plum. The feds came out in force with jeeps and guns and tried to lock him up for trespassing. And all he was trying to do was unwind fishing line from his propeller."

"That sucks," said Steve.

"My neighbor works there," said Rob. I'll give him a call and pick his brain."

"Maybe we should try the north side," I suggested.

"Too rocky," alerted Marty.

Steve looked worried. "You mean we're really

gonna do this?"

"Might as well," I said. "No guts, no glory,"

"And no grass," added Rob.

Chapter Thirty-One

At a little before eleven the next morning, I looked out the back window and saw Rob paddling up to my beach. "Hey," I yelled, going out to meet him. "You look exhausted."

"I left about an hour ago figuring I'd get here early. Didn't realize that the tide was so strong in this creek."

"Yeah. It's going out right now."

Marty moseyed over from next-door while Steve made his way down the driveway. We all sat down at the edge of the dock.

"Okay, men," said Marty, trying to sound like General Patton, "time for a strategy session. I think I found Socket's weed."

"How'd you do that?" asked Rob.

"Google Earth. I searched Plum Island by satellite all night and discovered an area that looks like a garden on the eastern side."

"That makes sense," I said. "The western part is too busy with the animal disease center, the federal offices and the ferry dock. Rob, did you talk to your buddy?"

"Yeah. He confirmed that the whole island is covered with surveillance cameras. The sandy south shoreline is watched the closest; our best bet would be to approach it from the north and stay on the east end. Stay away from the animal labs and kennels."

"Who's guarding the island?" asked Steve, nervously.

"Everybody and their mother," Rob muttered. "Homeland Security and the Federal Department of Agriculture have the jurisdiction on the land, but the surrounding waters are patrolled by the Southold Town Police, Suffolk County Police, New York State Police and sometimes the US Coast Guard."

"Jeez. And what about that guy, what do you call him, Timbo? Officer Wiz?" asked Steve apprehensively. "Do you think he's gonna be a problem, too?"

"Well, let's see," I said, stretching back on the heels of both hands. "For weeks now, we've been jerking him around. The other day we suckered him into Noyack Creek and left him stranded for three hours in low tide. Nah, I don't think he's got an issue with us at all."

"Shit," sighed Steve.

"Ahem," hacked Marty, bringing us back on task. "Here's my plan. We go over there at night, to the south side. The north side is too rocky, trust me, but we need one of those light-weight inflatables."

"Like a rubber duck boat?" asked Rob.

"Yeah," Marty said.

"I think I have one of those in my basement, next to Catey's old exercise ball. But I haven't used it in forty years. It's in the crawlspace, still wrapped in plastic."

"How'd you get that?" asked Rob.

"When I got out of college, my first job was assistant manager at a Consumers, that catalog shop, remember? It was the dot.com store of the 70's. I had a harem of high school girls working for me. We had this inflatable boat on display, which was leaking air, and my manager told me to toss it. So I did, right into the trunk of my old red jalopy. I'll pull it out later today and see if it still works."

"You do that," directed Marty and carried on. "I talked to a friend of mine in Massachusetts. His son grows medical marijuana and is expanding into the recreational market. If this stuff is any good, he'll give us up to forty grand for Socket's stash."

"Forty G's? That's a nice chunk of change—ten grand apiece," Rob shouted. He stood up and swayed his hips. "Hawaii, here I come."

"Or how 'bout a guys' fishing trip to the Keys? I suggested, getting up to dance with Rob. "We could troll for some beauties."

"I know what kind of beauties you're talking about," he jeered as he twirled me around.

"No really; I just want to catch a marlin, you know, to put up in my man-cave and get rid of the singing rubber bass."

Only he laughed at that one.

"We should give the money to Allie," Marty decided. "She's getting nothing out of her uncle's inheritance and needs to get those girls through college."

"You know, some of us can use the dough," grumbled Steve. "Not everyone has a New York City pension or a golden parachute."

"You're right," I agreed, not so much because I did, but because I wanted him to know I had his back.

"What? We're not keeping the money?" cried Rob, as he suddenly stopped his hula dance. Then he grinned. "Okay, easy come, easy go."

"This whole mission is not as easy as you might think," declared Marty. "First, we need to get two fully-grown plants. Second, one of them has to be flowering so they can check the THC levels. And third, we need to do this in the dark—and all without getting caught."

"This is going to be tougher than I figured," said Rob. "I think I'll need some of that brown stuff."

I ran into the house and returned with a small cooler filled with a local ale.

"Not exactly what I was thinking," said Rob, reaching for a cold one, "but this works."

"None for me," said Marty. "They got me on some heavy-duty pain meds for my back and I got PT in an hour. Give me a seltzer instead."

We took our first sips while Marty continued detailing his plan. "We need to do a trial run on Plum Island to locate Socket's farm before we do anything major."

Rob and I both nodded, but Steve just gulped away.

Marty soldiered on. "According to the fishing reports, guys are starting to catch black sea bass on the north side of Plum, and giant porgies are hitting on squid in eighteen feet of water, about thirty yards from the beach. One of us would have to brave the elements and swim to shore to locate the pot farm."

He and Rob automatically looked to me.

"Yes, sirs," I saluted, trying not to laugh.

"We go tomorrow at slack tide. It's easier without the currents."

Rob played along. "But, sir, the weekend forecast is for wind and rain."

"Then Monday it is. We'll take my boat," Marty

said, raising his glass of sparkling water in the air. "Lead me, follow me, or get out of my way."

Everything was set. Marty had the plan, Rob was itching to find the weed, and I was up for adventure. And Steve? He halfheartedly lifted his beer, contributing nothing but anxiety.

Chapter Thirty-Two

We all watched a struggling Marty get up from the chair and wobble home. "He looks like he's in pain," I said. "I'm gonna be in pain if I don't get going now," said Rob. "The tide is starting to turn." With that, he hopped into his kayak and paddled away.

I turned to Steve. "How's Ginny?"

He pulled another beer from the cooler. "Not so good. We got the results from the PET scan the other day. They found a mass on her ovary."

"Shit. That doesn't sound good."

"No. We got an appointment at Sloan tomorrow. They're gonna run more tests, probably get an MRI and take a biopsy and stuff."

"Sloan Kettering's the best hospital for cancer."

"Yeah. The thing is, it's not in my network. Even with Medicare and my supplement, this could cost me a ton of money."

"That's not good."

"Fucking Marty pisses me off sometimes. He's got more money than God and all the toys to boot. Has he even used those jet skis this summer?"

I shrugged.

"I'm pretty tapped out. I shouldn't have gotten the new boat. The dough from Socket's stuff would help, but I'm concerned about this crazy plan."

I sighed. "How's she holding up?"

"Good. She's scared, but who wouldn't be. We told the kids the other day. They're coming down this weekend, but we won't know much. They just want to see her."

"What can we do?"

"Nothing! There's nothing to do. I feel so fucking helpless."

He opened the cooler, but it was empty.

"Want me to get you another?"

"Nah. I should get going. Ginny needs me. Another beer and I'll be sleeping the afternoon away."

"You sure you're okay with this Plum Island deal?"

"Yeah, I guess so. It's a good distraction. But I'm nervous."

"Gotcha."

"But I could sure use the cash!"

Chapter Thirty-Three

The back door squeaked open. "What are you doing out here in the middle of the night?" asked Catey.

"I'm just thinking." I pointed upwards, "Look at that big, beautiful pumpkin." An orange tinted full moon stared back at us.

"You don't look too happy. What's going on, Mr. Sunshine?"

"I don't know. Life sure is fragile, isn't it? Unpredictable, too."

She sat down next to me and put a hand on my thigh.

"My three fishing buddies are getting old."

She nudged me with her elbow. "I hate to tell you this, Lovey, but so are you."

"But I'm lucky. The other day, Marty couldn't even get out of his chair."

"Yeah, Pam says his back is a real issue. He may need an operation."

"Ouch, that's so dangerous. If they nick the wrong nerve, he could be paralyzed for life. And my buddy Rob."

"How's he doing?" she interrupted.

"Weird, as always. The same guy who can remember the name of an obscure record from sixty years ago forgets to put bait on his hook. He drives me crazy."

Catey laughed. "Remember, they're both older than you."

I reached for her hand. "And Ginny…" I hesitated. "She . . . Ginny . . . ."

"What?"

"Ginny's got ovarian cancer," I blurted.

She froze. I pulled her closer and we sat silently.

"Steve told me something was wrong last week, but today it was definite. Supposed to keep it on the QT."

We sat there a few more minutes without speaking. A slight breeze blew in from the creek. She shivered. "I'm going in."

I could see she was holding back tears. "Right behind you."

I stared at the moon a few moments longer. The silence of the night was broken by the hoot of a neighboring owl. Looking up to a nearby tree, I could see the two bright eyes and the dark shape of the bird. My bare foot stepped on something soft and slimy. It was a slug. I was about to swat him, but I stopped.

Life is precious, I thought, even to a slug . . . or a jellyfish.

Chapter Thirty-Four

Fishing around Plum Island is always a challenge. Striped bass and bluefish dominate both the deep western channel called Plum Gut as well as the eastern rips called the Sluiceway and the Race. The north side is famous for blackfish, porgies and sea bass. Two poles are a necessity, and I was trying to decide which to bring when Steve showed up at Marty's dock that Monday in mid-August.

"Morning," I said. "Where's Rob?" I looked at Steve. "Weren't you supposed to pick him up?"

"He can't make it today. He fell."

"He fell?"

"That's what he texted me. He's on his way to the ER now."

"What happened?" I asked.

Steve shrugged. "Says he tripped."

"This isn't the first time," I said. "Last week he lost his balance and suddenly wiped out. The dock posts kept him from falling into the water or else he could have been seriously hurt. And have you noticed that bruise on his forehead?"

"What do you think is happening?" asked Marty.

"I'm worried about him," I said. "One of my close friends from school, his wife started falling a few years ago. She was not very athletic, more the cooking and sewing type, so their doctor gave her a script for PT and brushed it off. A year later, it turns out that she has the first signs of early Alzheimer's. They had recently retired and moved to a small house along Florida's intercoastal, and she just keeps getting worse and worse."

"That sucks," said Steve.

"My buddy says his wife stares at the TV all day, watching soap operas and game shows. They can't even have a normal conversation. Sometimes, she gets mad and has temper tantrums and tries to hurt herself. He has to wash her, dress her and feed her each day, plus now she's incontinent. The other day he called me, ecstatic, because he had figured out a way to keep her still so he could floss and brush her teeth."

"Doesn't he have help?" questioned Steve.

"He has a woman who comes in three mornings a week, but he uses that time for food shopping and errands. His kids fly down once in awhile, but it always ends badly. Last time she didn't even recognize them, and the sad thing is, it's only gonna get worse."

"The poor guy works his whole frigging life and *this* is his happy retirement!" Steve lamented.

"If I ever get that way," said Marty, "just walk next door and put a bullet in my head."

"Let's stop talking about this shit. It's way too depressing," said Steve. "Let's go find that pot."

We motored around the north side of Shelter Island, past Bug Light, and entered Gardiners Bay. As we approached the Orient Point lighthouse, we noticed a dozen or more boats drifting, but I couldn't stop thinking about Rob. That song that Elvis Costello wrote about his grandmother kept going through my head.

"I guess the stripers are around," said Steve. "We

may as well give it a shot as long as we're here."

"We got an hour to kill before slack tide," I said.

Fishing for striped bass in Plum Gut is a unique experience. During the day, the fish roam the bottom in eighty to one hundred feet of water, so you need a fourteen- or sixteen-ounce sinker just to keep your lure down. When they are hungry, a bucktail with a pork rind trailer will usually do the trick, but over the past few years, soft plastic baits in the shape of shads or minnows have become very popular. Live bait, such as herring, bunker and eel, also work, but they are best at night.

The tide was coming in so we made our way to the far side of the inlet and started our first drift through these dangerous waters. Steve rigged up his pole the traditional way with a bucktail, Marty put on a four-inch soft plastic shad, and I clipped on a diamond jig. The bottom of the Gut was a disarray of rocks and debris, and, if you were not careful, or just lazy, your lure would become another casualty of the ocean floor. This inevitably occurred at least once per trip.

On our second drift, we dropped our rods and as soon as mine touched the bottom, I got a strike. "Fish on," I yelled.

"What you got, Timbo?" asked Marty.

"Don't know yet, but it's fighting like a son of a bitch."

Marty brought up his lure and grabbed the net.

"I got one, too," Steve screamed from the stern.

I had my catch about halfway up when it started to run. The fish was getting tired and so was my arm. "It looks like a blue," I shouted.

Marty raced to the rear of the boat to help Steve,

who was reeling up fast. I pulled my fish over the rail and watched it flop around the deck. "Wow, that's one big fish," I gushed, unhooking the two-foot monster.

Bluefish are fun to catch. Baby blues, called snappers, abound in bays and creeks in the hot summer months and are the first fish caught by many a young angler. They swarm in large schools and are fierce fighters. When they attack a pod of baitfish on the surface, the water starts to boil and churn like a washing machine as the fish blitz their prey.

Bluefish are very traditional looking fish, like the kind a kid would draw, with a long head, a tapered body and a forked tail. They are blue-green and their mouths house two rows of extremely sharp teeth, and many fishermen have lost fingers to the jaws of these monsters. They're oily, and not everyone's favorite dinner, but the smaller, cocktail blues remind me of Friday nights in my Catholic home when I was growing up.

A memory erupted from years ago. I was helping out the lady next-door weed her garden. It was hard work for a nine-year-old, and when twelve o'clock came around, she would give me a couple of bucks and say, "Why don't you go down to the luncheonette and get yourself something to eat." Evelyn, behind the counter, took my order as I twirled around on the stool. When my hamburger, fries and egg cream arrived, a voice whispered, "Excuse me, son. You do know it's Good Friday? Don't you?" There, right behind me, was Father Flynn, unwrapping the cellophane from his pack of Camels. I picked up a fry, and I watched him walk out the door. After a few minutes, Evelyn asked, "Is there something wrong with your burger?"

"No," I said. "I can't eat it cause it's Good Friday."

"Well, if you don't eat it, I gotta throw it out. Don't think God would be too happy with you wasting food."

I looked at my burger. My first Christian dilemma. An easy choice, in retrospect, considering what lay ahead.

"Timbo," yelled Marty, startling me back to the moment. "Start the boat!"

We were in the chop, bobbing around at the mercy of the sea as waves crashed over the sides. He reached over the rail, bringing up a big striped bass in the net. I started the engine and steered us away.

"Nice fish," I yelled to Steve. "Keeper?"

"Yep. Twenty-nine inches, perfect size for grilling."

"Now, let's get out of here," said Marty. "Next stop, isle of the misfit grass."

We chugged our way around Pine Point heading east. Plum Island was shaped like a pork chop with an elongated tail. At its crux, where the tail starts, stands Fort Terry, built in 1897 and used in both World Wars as well as the Spanish American War, primarily because of its strategic location overlooking the entrance to Long Island Sound, the gateway to New York City.

"You know, Plum Island is kind of an eerie place," I said. "If you look at it on a map, it reminds me of the planet eater on an old *Star Trek* episode."

"I saw that one," said Steve. "It was called *The Doomsday Machine,* and I think Kirk nuked the frigging thing."

I smiled at him. "So, the jellyfish are still working."

"Some people say this island looks like a question mark," said Marty.

"I can see that," said Steve.

I started to chuckle.

"What are you laughing about?" asked Marty.

"It's the question mark thing, and it's real stupid and mean."

"Well, you can't leave us hanging."

"All right, there was this teacher in high school, taught Biology. He was older than dirt and had a bad case of curvature of the spine. We called him the 'the human question mark.'"

"Now that's effing mean," said Steve.

"I know, but he was old, and we were young."

"Well, he couldn't have been that old if he was still teaching, probably younger than us."

"You think that's mean?" said Marty. "So in college, we had this guy with cerebral palsy that we called Sparky. He was the nicest guy in the world, but when he walked, his metal crutches scraped against the cement and created—he paused for effect— sparks!"

"I can only imagine what those guys are saying about us," I said, pointing to a boatful of twenty-somethings fishing nearby. "Never in a million years would they believe what we old farts are really up to."

Marty stopped the boat and put down the anchor. I took off my shirt, put on my two-dollar water-shoes, and stood on the rail.

"I bet they think you're going in for a pee," Marty laughed.

"This'll show 'em," I shouted. I jumped up, grabbed my knees and cannon-balled into the water.

Marty and Steve started cracking up. "Rob would have loved this shit."

Chapter Thirty-Five

"Timbo made it," said Marty, relieved.

Steve squinted. "But why is he giving us the finger?"

"Look again, Mr. Magoo. He's giving us a thumbs up. He made it to the woods."

"Any chance he'll be caught trespassing?" asked Steve, a bit worried.

"Not today. It's pretty deserted around here," answered Marty. "It would be like finding a minnow in a school of bunker. Damn, I got something on my line."

"Well, bring it in. We might as well fish while Timbo explores."

"It feels like a porgy and it's fighting like one too."

Porgies are the Rodney Dangerfields of fish on the east coast. Also called scup, they are round-bodied bottom feeders, usually about a foot long, and they fight like crazy. They're also good to eat but have lots of bones. Traditionally scaled and cooked whole, the succulent meat is removed with a fork. Though easy to fillet, they yield only four strips of boneless meat, which can be breaded and fried, or sautéed in butter.

"What's the keeper size?"

"Nine inches."

"Well, that's easy to measure." Marty held the fish alongside his crotch and started to pull down his bathing suit.

"Dream on," Steve jeered.

"Are we keeping them?"

"Might as well. Rob uses them for fish cakes. He minces the fillets, mixes them in panko, eggs, onions and spices, and then puts them in the freezer. Eats them all winter."

Steve got a bite on his line.

"Here comes the police boat," Marty warned as Steve continued his battle with the fish. "Need the net?"

"I don't think so. It's definitely a porgy, but it's gotta be huge."

And huge it was, measuring seventeen inches and dwarfing its buddies in the live well.

The small Southold police boat was advancing. On board were two men sporting SPD baseball caps. "Ahoy, how goes the fishing today?"

"Actually, pretty good," responded Steve.

"We're here to do a random safety check. I'm Officer Smith and this is Patrolman Wizkowski." They tied their boat to the center cleat.

"Hello, Joe," said Marty. "Enjoying another sunny day on the water?" His question dripped with sarcasm.

Officer Wiz gave him a dirty look. "Do you have all your required equipment on board?"

Marty pulled out his life preservers and flares, held up a fire extinguisher, and pressed the horn button on his dashboard, perhaps a few seconds too long. "Do you need to see the registration?"

"I already checked it from the boat numbers. Do you guys all have fishing licenses?"

Marty removed his from the glove compartment and handed it to Joe.

"Mine's in my wallet," offered Steve.

"I trust you. Let's see what you got in the well."

"We just pulled up three porgies here and a striper in the Gut," said Steve, placing the catch on the deck.

"Nice fish." Officer Smith whistled as he eyed the striped bass. "How big?"

"Twenty-nine inches."

"What about the others?" questioned Wiz.

"They look good to me," said Smith.

"By the way, where are your other two buddies today?" Wiz asked.

"Rob's at the ER. He tripped this morning on his way over to my house."

"That's too bad. And what about Tim?"

All of a sudden, a yellow cigarette boat sped by, doing at least eighty miles an hour.

Look at that wake," interrupted Smith. "Better get in, Joe. We gotta go."

Officer Wiz barely made it back on board. Another lucky break.

****

The water was refreshing, about seventy-five degrees, perfect for cooling down on a hot summer day. I decided to stay underwater as much as possible in order to avoid surveillance. When I opened my eyes, I was dazzled by the abundance of fish, shells and plants. I knew that the probability of getting caught swimming to Plum Island was extremely rare, but why take a chance? I crawled to shore, scampered up a narrow path to a wooded area, and sat on a rock to rest and get my bearings. Staring at the southern shore, I was at the top of a small ridge with my back to our boat. In the distance was Gardiners Island. To my left and right were pine trees, water reeds and scrub vegetation.

"This is crazy," I thought to myself. "I'll never find a pot farm in this jungle. I'm not even sure what a pot plant looks like."

A few steps in, the landscape opened up. I could hear the rustling of small animals as I disturbed their quiet environment. Gazing at the undergrowth, I recognized beach plums, bayberry and chokeberry plants as well as balsam firs and red maples. The ground was a carpet of creeping juniper mixed with holly and dandelions, but nothing that looked like cannabis. A small lagoon with an outlet to the sea blocked my way forward.

Out of the blue, I heard the blast of a boat horn. Instinctively, I ducked, then quietly knelt on the ground and peeked through the underbrush. The red and blue insignia of the Southold Police Department was staring me in the face.

"Shit," I thought. "Where the hell are Marty and Steve? And what the hell do these cops want? This ain't good."

I looked around. "Stranded on Plum Island. No food. No water. Wonderful."

My stomach started to grumble. All of a sudden, a yellow cigarette boat sped by and the police started to move away. It was then that I saw my friends anchored off the shore. "They didn't ditch me after all."

Hoping Horace Greely had it right, I turned and headed west. After a few minutes, I began to smell a pungent odor, strong and musky, like old socks. I followed the scent and came upon a patch of pointed plants. I felt like Moses discovering the burning bush!

****

Marty and Steve still had their fishing poles in the

water when I climbed aboard.

"How'd you do?" asked Marty.

"Eureka," I smiled, removing the baggie from my pocket and holding it up.

"Holy shit, you really found it," cried Steve. "Where was it?"

"Behind some fir trees. It looked like a garden. It's spooky over there alone, but kind of exciting, too. I could sure use a beer."

Marty opened the cooler and served us each a crackling cold one. "Cheers!"

"What happened here?" I asked. "I saw the police and heard the siren go off."

"Oh, it was Officer Wiz busting our balls," Steve grumbled. "He claimed it was just a routine safety inspection, but Marty thinks otherwise."

"It sounds fishy to me," Marty said. "How the hell did he end up on the police boat? He goes back to work just a week ago, and now he's got a plum assignment like that?

"It's not really such a good gig," I said. "Ten hours on the water in the hot sun beats the shit out of you, and giving tickets to fishermen for keeping shorts and expired fire extinguishers don't make him Mr. Popularity."

"You're probably right," said Steve, reaching for another beer. "I can't believe Socket had a pot farm on Plum Island. That takes balls."

"Yeah, and smarts. Kept it compact, about a dozen plants a few feet high. Some had buds on them already." I opened up the sandwich bag and showed off my treasure. "Here, take a look."

Marty and Steve examined my stash and put

everything back in the bag while Steve asked, "How hard will it be to grab a few plants?"

"Not very. A few minutes with a shovel's all I need. Dig up two plants, put the whole shebang in a garbage bag, and we're in business. But we gotta do this at night."

"And we have to use Steve's boat," added Marty, "because it's got the best GPS."

Steve didn't look happy.

"And I need someone to go with me to play chickie."

Marty was quick to cop out. "I wouldn't be much help—with my bum shoulder and all."

Steve rolled his eyes and coughed.

"I'm sure Rob'll do it," I said, hoping to ease the tension. "He'd do anything to get his mitts on some pot." I rambled on. "So, how was the porgy fishing anyway?"

"It was okay," said Steve.

I opened the livewell and took a peek. "Wow, you got a few monsters in there, and our striper is still kicking. I'd say this is better than just okay."

We sat for a while bullshitting about the upcoming caper.

"Were you nervous when you heard the boat horn?" Steve asked.

"Not really, just shitting my pants. Actually, when I was traipsing through those reeds, I was thinking about Socket marching in the jungle. It's amazing, the fact that he saved those lives over in 'Nam and never told a soul."

"Must feel good to save someone's life," said Steve, a little too wistfully.

"Yeah, I saved someone's life just the other night," Marty boasted.

"You're a fucking bullshiter," snarled Steve.

"No it's true. I was walking the dog at dinnertime when I smelled gas. I noticed an open grill in my neighbor's garage. Two young guys were hanging out, and one was about to light up a smoke. So, I dropped Nellie's leash and ran towards them yelling 'Stop!' If he'd lit up that butt, that would have been the end. They were high as kites."

Listening to Marty's story, I flashed back to that summer day forty years ago. If only I had stopped to help those clammers.

****

"Earth to Timbo."

"Huh?"

"How about you?" asked Marty. "Did you ever save a life?"

"I did, but I'm not sure it counts. I was in high school, and I was walking home with a buddy of mine on this cold, cold night. We were coming back from a party at a girl's house in Bagel Bend. It must have been ten below zero; we were standing on the side of the road trying to light our cigarettes, when we spotted this thing by the curb. I thought it was an overturned garbage pail, but, as we got closer, we realized that it was a body of a kid a few years older than us."

"So whad'you do?" asked Steve.

"We knocked on a few doors, and, finally, a porch light came on. This man came out and helped us carry the guy inside, and then we went home. It turned out that the kid was a diabetic who lived a few blocks away. We didn't do much, but if we hadn't found him, he could have frozen to death."

"That's cool, Timbo," said Steve.

"How about you?" I asked.

"Yeah. It was back in high school; actually we had skipped school to go surfing at Seaside Park. A hurricane was coming up from the south and the waves were huge. They were big —ten, twelve footers—and the conditions were sloppy. I had my long board, a nine-eight nose-rider, and, after a half hour of paddling, I finally made it past the breakers. I looked around, and I was the only surfer out there. My buddies had all chickened out."

Steve was on a roll, and I was glad to see him so pumped up.

"I let about twenty big waves go by before I worked up the nerve to catch one. It was a quickie. I just dropped in, kicked out, but, boy, the adrenaline rush was amazing. I started to paddle back when I saw this surfboard blast off straight into the air and this kid in the water trying to get to it. Now this was long before bungee cords, so once you lost your board, you had to either retrieve it or swim to shore. Well, this guy wasn't swimming too well. After three or four strokes, his head dipped underwater, so I paddled over and picked him up, and the two of us managed to make it back to the beach. He had torn up his shoulder when he wiped out. He was about three years younger than me; years later, he became a really good surfer. I would see him around once in a while, and he would always introduce me as the guy who saved his life."

Steve sat there grinning.

"Good story," said Marty. "I'm sure it's all bullshit."

"Screw you."

Chapter Thirty-Six

We were back at Marty's dock. Out of my tackle box, I withdrew a long, sharp fillet knife.

"Are you going to kill me now or later?" joked Marty.

"No, you jackass. I'm going to clean the fish."

Steve began to spray down the rods as Marty hustled into his house. "Be right back," he yelled. "Nature calling. Again."

Steve strolled over. "I've never seen anyone fillet a porgy before."

"It's easy. You make a cut behind the head, and run your knife close to the spine, carefully removing the meat from both sides of the fish. Then you wedge the blade between the skin and the meat, and let the knife do its magic."

"Hey, you're pretty good at this."

"Catey says I got the touch of a sturgeon."

"Funny, except I don't feel like laughing much these days, especially when it concerns Ginny."

"I bet."

"I better get going; been away all day."

"Take your fish. Do you want some porgies, too?"

"Nah."

"We'll talk later," I said. "I'm going to run these over to Rob."

Marty opened the back door and watched as we

both left his yard.

"Hey, where you guys going? Was it something I said?"

I laughed. "Be back in a few. Gonna check on Rob." I started my car, and, in a few minutes, rolled into our buddy's driveway. Walking towards the house, I saw my pal on his front porch with a bandage on his elbow and an ice pack on his knee. "You okay?"

"Yeah, just a little banged up. I was carrying all my fishing stuff to the car this morning and I tripped on that lip where the driveway meets the brick path. I dropped everything and brought my hands up to protect my face and landed hard on my elbow. The last time I fell, I knocked out a tooth and the cost of the implant is draining my retirement fund."

"Did you go to the doctor?"

"Yeah, I went to the ER to appease Sue, but all I needed was a band aid and some ice." He suddenly turned serious. "Can I tell you something?"

"What's up?"

"I'm worried about what happened today. Losing my footing on a flat driveway is a recipe for disaster. I don't want to be one of those old guys who will be a burden on his kids."

"I know what you mean. The other day, when I was cleaning the gutters, my flip-flop got caught on a rung and I nearly killed myself. I got no sympathy from Catey, who reminded me, again, that I'm not thirty-nine anymore."

"That's funny. Sue said the same thing to me as I was walking out the door trying to juggle all my crap."

"Let me guess. You were carrying that old tackle box of yours? The one that weighs fifty pounds?"

He laughed. "Guilty as charged."

"If only we could stay young forever."

"You quoting Bob Dylan again?"

"No. Rod Stewart." I placed the bag at his feet. "I brought you some fish."

He peeked into the bag. "Porgies, my favorite. I'll spend the afternoon making fishcakes. We'll have some for dinner and I'll freeze the rest."

I sat down across from Rob and gave him the scoop on my visit to Plum Island and the guys' run-in with Officer Wiz.

"Boy, did I miss a hell of a day."

"Don't worry," I said. "The real fun is yet to come. Wanna be my wingman?"

"Hell yeah, Maverick. A few scotches before dinner and a couple ludes tonight, and I'll be good as gold in the morning."

"Good, because we might be going tomorrow."

****

After I started my car, I just sat there in Rob's driveway, thinking.

He's lucky. He could have fallen backwards, hit his head on the cement. Hell, he could've died. Damn that tackle box, probably filled to the brim with useless junk, much of it old and broken. But who am I kidding? I have one just like it, overloaded with sinkers, hooks, lures, bait and line. The handle is cracked, the latch is rusty, and the hinges squeak each time I open that ancient thing. Everything is packed in tightly, and I can never find what I'm looking for without dumping out all the stuff. Somewhere in that mess is my favorite pencil popper-—a rare gift from my dad-—yellow and black with two propellers and a treble hook attached to the rear. The lure is useless, but I just can't bear to throw it away. Like life, delicate and frail, it's still precious. Maybe when I'm gone, Kev will use my fishing box or Catey will turn it into a planter. Or maybe they will just throw it out.

I put the car in Drive and headed home.

Chapter Thirty-Seven

"Hey, you got something against sunscreen?" was the first thing out of Lucy's mouth when Joe entered Founders Pub.

"It's nice to see you, too," he said, taking his regular seat at the end of the bar.

"The usual?"

"Nah. I'll just have one of those," he said, pointing to the tap. "I'm trying to take it easy. Gotta work tomorrow."

"So how'd your face get so red, Icarus? Flying too close to the sun?"

"Icarus?"

"Oh, never mind."

"No, I'm working the patrol boat again. This morning they assigned me to the twenty-foot scout. No protection, not even a canvas top. I gooped myself up with SPF 30, but that didn't seem to help."

"Probably that white, Polish skin of yours. The sun fantasizes about guys like you."

"Well, at least someone is fantasizing about me."

"Seriously, you're gonna burn your way to a major case of melanoma before the summer ends."

"Nobody would care."

"You're an ass," said Lucy, shaking her head. "Go to the pharmacy, buy yourself some good sunscreen, SPF50 or higher. You want some food?"

"I'll have the Tavern Burger, but without the fries."

"Do you want a side salad?"

"Sure, Italian dressing on the side."

She rolled her eyes. "Salad, no fries and light beer; what is happening to the old Joe we all know and love?"

"The old Joe wasn't doing it for me—or anyone else. It's time for a change. If nothing else, maybe I'll lose a few pounds."

She placed a second beer on Joe's coaster, brought over his dinner, and moved to the other end of the bar.

Joe ate in silence and started to review his new police manual with one eye on the TV blaring the Mets' game. Lucy returned to take the plates away. "Another?' she asked, pointing to the empty.

"I better not. I got another long day on the water tomorrow."

"How about some coffee? I just brewed myself a fresh pot."

"Now that sounds perfect."

Lucy came back with two steaming mugs, placing one in front of him, alongside a small pitcher of cream and a variety of sweeteners. She watched carefully as Joe ripped open three sugars and emptied the contents into his drink. He took a sip and slowly reached for another packet.

"Boy, you sure know how to ruin a good cup of coffee. If cancer doesn't get you, diabetes will."

"It's my only vice. You know, being on the water isn't as much fun as it used to be. Busting chops and counting life preservers is not very exciting in the grand scheme of things."

"Neither is changing kegs and mixing drinks," she

muttered, "but it pays the bills."

Joe smiled and lifted his cup. "You got that right."

Chapter Thirty-Eight

The next day was hot and breezy when Marty and I met for our morning ritual. "This wind is supposed to crank up a notch overnight, but tomorrow looks calm and clear," I said.

"How come Steve gets his weather from a hot chick on TV and I get you?"

"Cause I'm right and they're not. *Salut.* I raised my jellyfish and placed it on my tongue, as Marty swallowed his whole, washing it down with a bottle of orange juice.

"Drinking healthy this morning, I see."

"Pam's got me putting together some furniture today, so I figured a screwdriver would come in handy."

"Marty stop. You're killing me."

He laughed. "We still on for tomorrow night?"

"Yep. It's gonna be a late one. Slack tide is about twelve."

"Rob on board?"

"Says no way he would miss this one—even if it kills him."

****

I sat down on my dock looking out at the water, wondering about what really happens when you die. My parents were devout Catholics and had a strong faith that I always admired. I'm sure that when their time was up, they entered their Heaven. Friends of mine insist that when you take your last breath, everything just shuts off. Kaput! I can't imagine that all these thoughts, ideas and dreams rumbling around in my brain will just disappear—go away forever. What a waste. I like to think that the journey continues, that somehow this good energy mysteriously finds its way into new beginnings. Plants do it, some animals do it, heck, even humans do it. Hair, skin, nails. Why not our souls? Maybe life after death is an even bigger adventure.

Hey, maybe a chance for a do over.

Chapter Thirty-Nine

Officer Wiz was in the locker room when the sergeant came by and tapped him on the shoulder. "Chief wants to see you."

One of the other cops swiped a finger across his neck in a slicing motion, and Joe gulped. He finished dressing and hustled into the boss's office.

"Close the door and sit down, Joe."

"Yes sir."

"Have you seen this?" Chief Barkley tossed him the latest copy of the *Suffolk Times*.

"No sir. I haven't had a chance to read it yet."

"Check out page four."

Joe opened the paper and saw the headline. *Boater Protest Planned for Plum Island Beaches*. Then, he looked up.

"What's your take on this?" asked the Chief.

"They've been talking about this for years, Ed. Since the land is federal property, people think it should be open to the public."

"Well, I just got word that the protest is imminent. I need to add more patrols to the water. Pronto."

Joe quietly breathed a sigh of relief. He wasn't getting canned.

"You know these waters better than anyone. Are you okay taking on some extra shifts?"

"Sure thing, Chief."

"Good. I'm going to put you on the big boat. If nothing else, it will get you out of the sun."

Joe chuckled. "That'd be great."

Wiz strolled out of the office smiling. "Maybe my luck has finally changed," he said under his breath. "Could be the beginning of a brand new day."

Chapter Forty

I topped off the inflatable with air and stuffed the whole thing, along with the oars, fishing poles and tackle box, into the bed of Marty's big ass pick-up truck. "I brought some beer, water and sandwiches," I said, helping him load the cooler. "This could be a long night."

We pulled up to Steve's house a few minutes later and carted the rubber dinghy and all of our other crap onto his boat. "That's bigger than I thought," said Steve, pointing to the raft. "Where we gonna put it?"

"Normally," I said, "we would tie it on the front of the bow, but that may cause suspicion."

"Oh, you think?" said Steve, a bit too sarcastically. "Striper fishing at night in a rubber boat? What happens if we pull up a forty-pounder?"

I grinned. "Then it'll be tight with two guys and a fish jumping around."

Sounding a little apprehensive, Steve sighed. "I don't even know why we're doing this."

"It's the right thing to do for Socket's niece," said Marty. "He'd appreciate it."

"For the weed," said Rob. "And so that that Officer Wiz guy doesn't get his paws on the stuff first."

"Because we can," I said. "Think of all the stuff we can't do anymore."

"Like going to bed without getting up three times

to pee," cried Marty.

"Or getting it up all night long," I twerked.

"Amen to that," echoed Rob.

Steve was growing impatient. "Just put the damn thing on the deck."

"I'll sit up top," I said, stepping around the railing to reach the bow, and Rob followed me, both of us wanting to avoid a scene.

We loosened the dock lines and headed out to sea. The sky was clear, the temperature was in the eighties, and there was a slight breeze from the west. The moon was entering its third quarter so there would be enough natural light to help us navigate our way. Steve grabbed the wheel with two hands and Marty played co-pilot, watching for buoys. The GPS wrote a trouble-free track across the bay.

Rob turned to me with a smile. "I can remember doing crazy things like this when I was a kid. In high school, my brothers and I broke into the stables at Van Courtland Park and tried to take the horses for a ride. It was a warm night, like tonight. We brought bunches of carrots, jumped a stockade fence, and lured the horses out into the paddock. Then we tried to mount them!"

"Without a saddle?"

"Yeah, like Tonto! My one brother hopped on an old nag and rode her around for a while. He finally fell off and landed on his ass. We were whooping and hollering; after a while, the lights went on and security guards started blowing their whistles and running in all directions as we escaped into the night. We got on the number 4 train to get home, when all of a sudden we sensed an awful smell. Our sneakers were caked in horseshit."

"Whoa, bet that car cleared out fast," I said. "That reminds me of my pool hopping days on hot summer nights. My friends and I would sneak out of our houses, usually after midnight, and jump into other people's backyard pools. Sometimes, there were seven or eight of us and we had to be real quiet. Every once in a while, the homeowners would wake up, turn on the lights and half-heartedly chase us away."

"Did you ever get caught?"

"No, but one time this man opened the door and his dog crashed through the screen after us. It's amazing how fast you can get yourself over a six-foot chain link when a hundred- pound German Shepherd's on your tail."

We had just passed Bug Light and watched the summer sun set over the Ram's Head Point on Shelter Island. A few fishing boats were returning, done with the evening bite. Steve's boat was still on plane, and the smooth ride continued even in the choppy waters of Plum Gut.

"Let's go around the island to check for trouble before we start this venture," advised Marty.

"Hey, about time you had a good idea," cracked Steve.

We rode through the Gut, up the north side of the island. As we rounded the east end, all looked normal. Suddenly, we spotted the headlights of a vehicle coming straight towards us.

"Oh shit," Steve said, pointing. "What do you think that is?"

"No worries," Rob assured us. "Probably just security making their rounds. They do it every few hours,"

Sure enough, the lights changed from white to red as the car turned around.

"According to our GPS, this is the spot directly in line with the path I found the other day," explained Marty. "It's now or never."

Steve hesitated for a moment, then flipped the switch to drop the anchor. I tossed the inflatable over the side and held it close so Rob could climb on board. "Whoa!" he cried.

"Jesus Christ, you almost tipped it over," said Steve, as Rob struggled with his balance.

I followed without issue as Marty gave us a folded shovel and some garbage bags. "Hold on," he said, "you don't want to forget these," handing us a couple of pink, plastic flashlights, complete with stars and sparkles, probably pilfered from his granddaughters' stash. "Remember, two blinks when you're ready to be picked up."

I laughed. "If we get caught, the cops are gonna love these."

Chapter Forty-One

The inflatable was wobbly. I took a kneeling position in the front as the lookout, and Rob, his back to the bow, started rowing. "This thing cuts through the water pretty smoothly. I can't believe that it has oarlocks," he remarked.

"Oh yeah, this was the top seller at the store back in the day," I said with nostalgic pride.

After a few minutes, we reached the shallows and made our way to the beach. I noticed a pile of driftwood about ten yards to the right and decided to hide the raft there.

"Good idea," said Rob.

We put the boat on the ground and covered it with sticks and brush. A couple of clouds passed overhead so we sat on the beach, waiting for our eyes to adjust to the dark.

"I can't see my hand in front of my face," said Rob.

"Don't worry; things will start to focus in a while. I don't want to use the flashlight if I can help it."

"Got it, Timbo."

The moon came out of hiding. We started to walk quickly, keeping close to the ground, going away from the shore to a wooded area. Rob sat on the beach as I scurried around in all directions looking for familiar landmarks from my recent recognizance. I finally found the path, but as I made my way towards it, my foot hit a log and I stumbled, landing flat on my face. "Oh shit!"

Rob's flashlight immediately lit up the area.

"Turn that fucking thing off," I hissed. Little did I know that the damage had already been done.

"Timbo, are you okay?"

"Just pissed. I scraped my knee and lost my flashlight. But the trail is right here; just follow me."

I made my way in the direction of Socket's garden. The travel was slow, but every so often, the moon would peak through the clouds, allowing us to double our pace for a moment, until the darkness descended again.

"I can smell the plants," smiled Rob.

Sure enough, a hemp-like odor soon filled the air. A few moments later, we found ourselves staring at the batch of marijuana plants.

"Wow!"

Even though I couldn't see Rob's face, I imagined his grin was as wide as a kid's on Christmas morning. The silence was broken by the loud wails of a siren, unlike those of the familiar police horn or fire whistle, but rather short, irritating bursts like the ones of police cars in European movies.

"I don't like the sound of that," said Rob.

"Me neither." There was a scurrying in the bushes. "I don't think the natives liked it either." I noticed a light on the water, so I pointed to it.

"Shit, there's a searchlight on that vessel and it's coming our way," whispered Rob.

Sure enough, a boat, slowly making its way up the coast, was shining a large beam on the shore. "Our flashlight must have triggered some alarms," I said.

"Sorry."

"Not your fault. It could have been a motion detector."

"What do we do now?"

"I have an idea. Stay close behind me."

We doubled back on the trail, me leading the way. I calculated that we still had a few minutes before the searchlight discovered Steve's boat.

"Do you think Marty and Steve will stay where they are?"

"Why not? They're not doing anything illegal, just fishing."

"Yeah, but everyone knows there are no fish where we're anchored."

"Not everybody, just fishermen. Shine the light to the right, over there, by that red maple tree."

"Got it."

I carefully climbed my way down. Around the base of the tree was a thick string—no— a crab line. I started pulling on the rope and presto. Out of the water came a metal cage a bit larger than a football.

"Is that a killie trap?"

"No, even better. It's an eel trap!"

"Eels, of course," said Rob. "Everyone knows that the best way to catch a striped bass is to live-line a fresh eel at night."

"Everyone is right, including the men who work at Plum Island," I said. "What do you think the night shift guys do on their four a.m. lunch break?"

"They fish?" he asked incredulously.

"Of course they fish." I carried the trap over and handed it to Rob. "Here. Take this. I hate eels. They're the snakes of the sea, slimy and impossible to attach to a hook. Whenever I pick one up, it always finds a way to wrap itself around my arm."

"You have to knock them out," advised Rob. "Grab them in the center of their bodies and bash their heads against the boat rail. It stuns them and makes it easy to get the hook in their mouths."

"Yeah, tried that; only seems to make them mad. Anyway, go back to the boat and take the trap with you. If anyone asks what you were doing on the island, tell them that you were just getting eels. Let's hope they know that fresh bait from local waters is the best way to catch local fish."

We started walking back.

"What about you, Timbo?"

"I'll stay here, dig up the plants, and figure out a way to get off the island. If these guys are catching eels, there must be a kayak or canoe around here somewhere."

When we reached the beach, I could see a large boat docked next to Steve's. "Are you okay with this, Tonto?"

"More than okay, Kemosabe."

"Great. Tell Marty and Steve that if they don't get locked up, they should wait for me on the eastern shore. And remember, two blinks of the flashlight!"

Chapter Forty-Two

The deafening sound of a blaring siren pierced the quiet of the night.

"What the hell is that?" cried Steve. "Fuck! I think someone's on to us."

"That bright light on the beach may have triggered a sensor or something," said Marty.

"On this deserted part of the island? Why the hell do they need that kind of sophisticated security around here?"

"It's the Federal Government. They love to waste money on shit like that."

"What do we do now?" panicked Steve.

"We stay here and fish," said Marty.

"Nobody fishes here," Steve snapped back.

"Calm down. There's nothing illegal with fishing off of Plum Island. What's your problem anyway?"

"It's my fucking boat. That's my problem."

"Stop being such a wuss."

"And what happens if Rob and Timbo get caught?"

"They'll figure something out."

A large boat with a flashing red light came into view around the eastern tip of Plum Island. On its bow was a searchlight shining at the beach and the woods. "That's a big boat," said Marty. "I wonder who it belongs to?"

"Well, looks like we're gonna find out real soon."

The searchlight settled on Steve's boat.

"Talk about blinded by the light," said Marty. "I feel like I'm back on the stage."

"You're an actor?"

"Yeah."

"Figures. Every actor I know is an asshole."

It was a big boat, thirty-five feet, at least, with twin 300 horsepower engines and a flying bridge. Custom made for police work. The searchlight suddenly went dark and was quickly replaced by a smaller spotlight. The pilot expertly moved alongside Steve's boat and a voice hailed out. "Ahoy there. What are you doing out this way?"

"Fishing," yelled Marty.

"Permission to come aboard," said the unknown voice. "U. S. Department of Homeland Security."

"By all means," gulped Steve.

Instantly, standing in the middle of the deck, appeared a large, uniformed man dressed in black. "Special Agent Frank Cavaliere. We're investigating a disturbance on Plum Island. Can I please see some identification?"

"Here's my license and boat registration," Steve said and handed them over to the officer.

"There have been reports of illegals being smuggled down from Canada," Cavaliere said. "These islands, Plum, Gull and Fisher's are being used as overnight points for the cargo."

"Cargo!" said Marty, incensed, his face turning red. "Illegals are now considered cargo?"

Before Steve could stop him, Marty continued his rant. "These are human beings. Mostly hard-working folks, looking for a better life. Like our forefathers did."

"Sorry," said Cavaliere. "I didn't mean to be unsympathetic. Just shoptalk."

Right then, they heard a big splash.

"What was that?" the fed asked, turning his spotlight on the approaching inflatable. "Is he with you?"

"Yeah," stammered Steve.

There was Rob, rowing against the current, the big, ugly tongue in the center of his black tee shirt lit up by numerous flashlights.

"He's not moving very quickly," said Steve. "I think the boat is losing air."

The three observers watched as the rubber craft pulled up next to Steve's rig. "Hi, guys," Rob said, cool as a cucumber. "I see we have company."

"Frank Cavaliere, Department of Homeland Security."

"Nice to meet you. I'm Rob, retired fireman and sometimes fisherman. Hey, you're not related to Felix Cavaliere, the lead singer of the Young Rascals are you?"

"What? No!"

Rob held up the large silver container. "I've got the goods."

Steve groaned. "Oh great."

"Could somebody give me a hand here?" Rob asked. "I think I sprang a leak."

Steve steadied the rubber boat while Marty helped pull Rob on board.

Rob placed the cage on a seat and reached for a towel. "Now what was that hit song of theirs?" he wondered out loud.

"Hand that over," ordered the fed. He picked up the

trap and turned it over. A small clasp in the center held the two sides together.

"Don't touch that," Marty yelled, a second too late, as the container popped open and everyone watched in horror as a bunch of huge, slimy eels escaped from captivity and landed on the floor of the boat.

Agent Cavaliere's hand instinctively went for his gun but stopped short of firing when Rob blurted, "Don't shoot! They're innocent!"

Marty started laughing and Steve scrambled to collect the escaped creatures. "Don't just stand there. Help me pick these suckers up before they ruin my boat."

Cavaliere grabbed one, barehanded. As it slid through his fingers, he asked, "Do they bite?"

"Shit yeah!" said Rob.

The cop dropped the eel like a hot potato, and everybody laughed out loud, even Steve. He was still picking up eels when the Southold Police Boat pulled up. The interior light switched on and there on the deck stood Officer Wiz! "Hey, guys!"

"Hi, Officer," said Marty.

Steve and Rob nodded.

"What are you old salts up to now? Smuggling?"

"Just fishing," stammered Steve.

"And who's this?" inquired Wiz with a nod for the fed.

"Special Agent Frank Cavaliere, Department of Homeland Security." Frank pointed at Rob. "This one here was navigating back from Plum Island. Federal jurisdiction presides over that area."

"I just went to get the eels," Rob whined. "No law against that, is there?"

"We got a tip that someone is hiding illegal immigrants on these small islands," the agent explained, mostly to Wiz. "Thought we had a pick-up in progress,"

"Listen, I know these three geriatrics personally," Wiz assured him. "I can guarantee you that they are not trafficking illegals. Their wives probably threw them out of the house tonight."

"Why not buy eels at the bait store?" asked Cavaliere.

"Local eels for local fish," said Rob. "Anytime you can get an advantage over the fish, it's worth it, and striped bass are smart fish."

"That sounds fishy to me," said the fed. "How can I be sure?"

"That's the name of the song," yelled an excited Rob.

"Trust me," said Wiz. "These guys are harmless, and though they're a pain in my ass, they're not criminals."

On that note, Agent Cavaliere bid his farewell and returned to the big boat. "I'm required to finish my perimeter search," he said.

Officer Wiz turned to Marty. "Where is your fourth wheel tonight?"

"He had something more important to do."

Chapter Forty-Three

Under a starry, starry night, I sat on the beach and watched Rob stumble into the water, then hop into the inflatable. I knew that the bottom of the raft was probably resting on the sand, so I prayed that gravity and friction wouldn't cause it to spring a leak. I retraced my steps along the path to Socket's farm. The clouds had vanished, and a bright moon lit up the whole area. I quickly excavated a few plants and put them into the black garbage bag along with an extra shovelful of soil.

"Now to find some transportation," I said.

Stash in hand, I made my way to the beach, searching for a way to get back to the boat. Not a kayak, canoe or float in sight. On to plan B. I tossed the bag containing the pot into a second garbage bag and started to blow it up. After ten minutes of strenuous exertion, I had me a huge homemade float. "I'm a regular Robinson Crusoe," I mused.

I knew I had to wait for the coast to be clear before I could swim back. I figured it was almost ten o'clock, and I thought the best time to make my move would be around midnight. Slack tide today was set for 2350 hours, when the water would be the calmest. I sat down, closed my eyes, as memories of a past incident flooded my mind.

It was the mid-eighties, and I was returning from a Chicago trade show on a 707 jet. I'd just spent a whole week manning my company's booth at the National Plastics Show and had become friendly with our neighbors, who represented a Japanese company trying to break into the U.S. prophylactic market. My boss Tony and I were sitting in the last row of the smoking section, while we waited for the plane to take off.

Bored and a little bit drunk, Tony pulled out a handful of rubbers from his pocket, gave me a few and told me to blow them up. When we had a bunch, we launched them like beach balls towards first class. They were huge, about two feet in diameter. The whole plane was full of men, and everybody got into it, making sure the inflated condoms never touched the floor. Everyone was hooting and laughing when suddenly a stewardess came out from behind the black curtain and barked, "Gentlemen, what is going on here? We are not taking off until you put your toys away."

She was pretty, statuesque and reminded me of Nurse Ratched from *Cuckoo's Nest*. A collective groan exhaled from the mouths of the deflated passengers, who popped the big rubber balloons with their pens and Swiss army knives. How things were different twenty-five years ago.

It was starting to get chilly, so I got up to stretch and was startled by the sound of a muffled sneeze.

Chapter Forty-Four

"That was close," said Steve.

"I can't believe that jackass Cavaliere went for his gun," said Rob.

"The whole thing was pretty comical," chuckled Marty, "especially when the eels were squirming all over the floor."

"Comical to you maybe. Everything is comical to you these days," griped Steve.

"What's your problem?"

"Nothing you'd understand."

"We'd still be there if it wasn't for Officer Wiz showing up and saving our sorry asses," Rob wisecracked, easing the tension.

"He didn't save us," said Marty. "We weren't doing anything wrong."

"You're an ass," said Steve. "Rob was trespassing on federal property. Duh!"

"Trespassing, that's petty bullshit. What's with you today? Why'd you even bother coming?"

"Good question."

Marty turned to Rob. "Does Timbo have a plan?"

"He's looking for a kayak or canoe. He figures whoever set those eel traps must have a boat somewhere around there. Said he'll signal us from East Point when he's ready."

Within a few minutes the three fishermen were

drifting off the end of the island.

"As long as we're here waiting, do you think it would be okay to drop a line in the water?" asked Rob. "I wouldn't want these beautiful eels to go to waste."

"I guess," said Steve, grudgingly. "But as soon as we see Timbo's signal, we gotta go."

"Great," said Rob. I'm going to try without a weight, maybe grab a fish close to the surface."

"I'm going deep," said Marty. "We're in sixty feet of water, so an eight-ounce sinker should be enough."

With a rubber glove, Marty picked up an eel and rapped its head against the rail. The sea snake instantly stopped moving, and Marty expertly inserted the hook through its mouth and dropped it into the water.

"Can I borrow that glove?" asked Rob. He put it on his hand, grabbed an eel, slammed its head on the side of the boat, hooked it and watched as the lifeless bait headed into the ocean.

"I think you killed it," said Marty. "If not, it's definitely brain damaged."

The tide was moving slowly so the weight was doing its job.

"I think I got something," said Marty, excitedly. "No, wait; I'm stuck on the bottom."

"Jerk can't tell the bottom from a fish," mumbled Steve under his breath.

Marty kept reeling. "Shit, it *is* a fish, and it feels like a big one."

Rob took up his line to open space for Marty. The fish made four or five sprints away from the boat and then suddenly broke the surface.

"Holy shit," screamed Rob. "That's a beauty!"

"Dinner tomorrow night," sang Marty.

Just as Rob reached for the net, two bursts of light came from the eastern point of the island. "That's the signal from shore," said Steve. "We gotta go."

Marty continued to reel as Rob stood by, net in hand. The striper saw the boat and made one last dash for freedom.

"We gotta go, now," shouted Steve.

Marty kept reeling when, all of a sudden, the line snapped, throwing him back on his heels. "Shit."

There stood Steve, knife in hand. Marty dropped his pole and started towards him, his fists flying. "I'm gonna fucking kill you!"

Rob grabbed Marty around his waist. "It's only a fish," he said.

Steve reached for a crunch bar and started the boat.

Chapter Forty-five

I walked over to the bushes and turned on Rob's flashlight.

"Please, *Señor*," said a soft, nervous voice. Out of the brush came a young woman, probably in her twenties, holding the hand of a dark-haired boy about six. Her green eyes peered out of a worn hoodie.

"Three days, no food," she said, and then she started to cry. "Please, *Señor*," she said again, "help us."

"Don't cry. I will help you. What is your name?" I asked, turning to the boy.

"Carlos. And this is my mother, Maria."

"I'm so sorry. I can't help you right now, but I promise I will come back to get you."

"Please, *Señor*, don't leave us," cried Carlos.

"Please, help us," echoed his mother.

"I promise I will be back," I said, picking up my black balloon full of goods. I started walking away, stopping only to signal Steve's boat. From a hundred yards returned two flashes of light.

I tied the bag around my waist, walked into to the chest-deep water, and started to swim. Surprisingly, the Sluiceway was flat, like a sheet of glass, very unusual for this area. I glided towards my destination with my glad bag floating next to me. I switched to the sidestroke, glanced behind me, and saw the two castaways jump in the water.

****

Rob returned the signal and the guys prepared for the pick-up. Steve kept the engine running at trolling speed, trying to keep the boat stationary. The humming of the motor prevented everyone from hearing the sound of any paddling. Rob was scanning the coast with his flashlight looking for me, when I shouted out, "Over here."

There I was on the side of the boat with my big bag and two swimmers in tow.

"Hey Timbo, you made it," said Rob.

"Who are they?" growled Steve, pointing to Carlos and Maria.

"Just get us out of the water, will ya?"

"Well, get on board," said Rob, reaching out with a hand.

"Not so fast," said Steve.

"Would you please just get us on board," I yelled. "It's friggin'cold."

I hopped aboard and watched Maria and Carlos climb on to the swim platform with Rob's help.

"Are they illegals?" asked Steve.

"I didn't ask. I told them that I would come back for them, but they decided to follow me."

Steve turned and stared at me. "So now they're my fucking problem?"

"Calm down," I said. "I'll just row them off to safety on the inflatable. We can't just leave them."

"Steve, you can't be serious," said Rob. "They must be starving. The least we can do is offer them food and water."

"What's wrong with you?" glared Marty, staring

straight at Steve.

"What's wrong with me? You fucking want to know what's wrong with me? Everything. Here I am, out on my fucking boat, chasing down some illegal pot plants for you guys. Meanwhile, my life is going to shit."

"Then you shouldn't have fucking come out today. What's pissing you off?"

"Nothing you'd understand rich boy with the perfect life."

"Whoa, whoa buddy!"

Rob started to say something when Steve blurted out, "Fuck it. Just get them in the boat."

Rob went over and put his arm around Steve. "I can't see how helping them stay alive could be construed as smuggling."

"Fine. Just help them on board until we figure out what to do."

"This is Maria and her son Carlos," I said.

Steve nodded.

Rob handed each of them dry towels and bottles of water. "*Hola*," he said to Maria and suddenly a rush of Spanish sounding words erupted from her mouth as quickly as tears gushed from her eyes.

"*Mas despacio, por favor*," said Rob, and Maria repeated her words much more slowly.

I moved closer to Steve and lowered my voice. "Sorry. I didn't mean to put you in this predicament. I tried my best to discourage them, but I think that they're just really scared."

He nodded again. "So am I. It's my boat. I'm the person who could get into real trouble here. If we get caught, it could turn ugly and costly for me. I don't know if I could handle one more thing with all the shit I'm going through."

"I know. I'm sorry."

Marty reached into the cooler and handed Carlos a ham sandwich. "You look hungry. Go ahead, eat."

"Thank you," he smiled and gave half to his mother. After a few bites, Carlos pulled off his wet T-shirt, and I noticed a chain with a silver medal around his neck.

"Hey, is that a Saint Christopher medal?" I asked. His smile grew wider. "I used to have one of those. Where'd you get it?"

"My dad gave it to me," he said, taking it off to show me the engraving on the back.

I pretended to read the small print, grinned, then returned the precious necklace to Carlos as he continued to devour his sandwich.

As the two guests ate their food, Rob came over and gave us the scoop. "Maria is from El Salvador. She and her husband, Juan, were smuggled into Texas. Six months later, Carlos was born. Maria cleaned houses and Juan worked as a roofer, until he fell off a ladder and died. That's when mother and son decided to move to Greenport to live with her uncle. A friend who's a long-haul trucker picked them up in El Paso and drove them to Rhode Island. Her uncle hired someone to meet them and take them across the Long Island Sound, but when the storm hit the other day, the guy chose to wait it out on Plum Island. Maria and Carlos slept on the beach that night, and when they woke up, the man, the boat and all their possessions were gone. The uncle has been waiting for her phone call."

Maria removed a flip phone wrapped in plastic

from her shorts, looked at it and sighed. "Dead."

Steve looked to Marty. "If I take them on the boat, all the way to Greenport, am I helping her with an illegal immigration into the US?"

"Possibly."

"Great. Between harboring illegals and hiding your fucking plants, I'm screwed."

"Maybe not," said Marty, instinctively kicking into lawyer mode. "If we drop them off at the closest land mass, then technically, we never took them anywhere, just returned them to the nearest beach. Perhaps the uncle could meet them there."

"Fine," agreed Steve, exasperated, but secretly grateful.

Rob handed Maria his cell phone and turned to Carlos, "Tell your mom to call her uncle. Let him know that you're both safe and ask him to pick you up at Orient Point."

Maria placed the call and, after a few rings, a smile of relief crossed her face. Clearly her uncle had answered the phone. As she chatted in rapid-fire Spanish, she questioned Rob about the details, then relayed instructions into the phone.

After Maria hung up, she said something to Carlos, who turned to me. "He will meet us."

"Oh shit," cried Steve. "We gotta go right now. Here comes a boat."

Chapter Forty-six

Sure enough, there on the horizon, a spotlight was heading our way. Marty took charge. "Rob, get those two up front. Put them on the floor between the seats. Timbo, you may have to hide, too. Can you fit in the head?"

"I don't think so. These plants take up the whole room. I'll just lie down on the deck."

Rob helped Maria and Carlos get around the cabin; as they made their way to the bow, Steve started the engine. Soon we were gliding through the waters of Gardiners Bay on our way to Orient. The other boat was about a half mile away on a collision course with us. Steve kept the craft steady at twelve knots.

"I think it's that Southold police boat again," Rob hollered.

Marty turned to Steve. "Where the fuck are you going?"

The vessel started to rock up and down with the waves. "I'm just following the GPS."

"Well, you just followed the damned thing into the middle of Plum Gut. Slow the fuck down."

As Steve threw the engine into Neutral, the boat lurched forward. "Then you fucking drive, asshole!"

"The police boat is almost here," I yelled.

"Police. Oh shit," shouted Rob.

When the boat slowed down, Carlos jumped up.

"Get down," whispered Maria.

But he was already on the seat cushion heading towards the console. "My medal! I left it on the cooler. I have to get my medal."

Once he had his treasure securely around his neck, he hopped up to the deck and grabbed for the handle, but the boat rocked. He lost his grip and disappeared into darkness.

"Carlos!" Maria screamed.

I kicked off my sandals, stood on the rail, and dove in after him.

Not this time, I decided.

Chapter Forty-Seven

I surfaced a moment later in the explosive waters of Plum Gut. The water was cold and the tide was ripping. I opened my eyes but everything was pitch black.

Plum Gut is located east of Orient Point and west of Plum Island. The riptide here is turbulent and treacherous, even on a calm day. I heard crying on my left and started swimming towards the sound.

"Carlos," I yelled.

"Here," came a weak response.

I swam fast. A beam of light slowly moved across the surface of the water and finally found the small, bobbing head. I swam even faster. A moment later I grabbed Carlos under his arms and held him up, all the while treading water the way I learned in Boy Scouts.

He was hysterical. He grabbed me by the neck, wailing, "I'm sorry."

"Carlos. I got you."

"Mama, mama."

"Carlos, calm down. Breathe."

"Mama."

I finally got him under control. We were drifting fast toward the rocks surrounding the Coffee Pot. Suddenly there were two lights on us. I looked back and saw Steve's boat side by side with the Southold PD unit.

"What's taking them so long?" I thought.

As the light was blinding me, I turned away. My legs were getting tired and starting to cramp. The water was cold. Carlos was getting heavy.

"Mama."

I heard the sound of a motor and a woman screaming. I kept pumping my legs up and down, up and down.

"Mama," Carlos cried as his body shook from the cold.

I heard a splash to my left. "Shit. I hope there are no sharks around."

"*Medusa grande*," Carlos screamed.

"Jellyfish? Oh shit," I thought. "Probably seeking revenge."

****

"Oh shit," Steve muttered and shut off his engine.

Maria stood up and screamed just as Rob grabbed her around the waist and anchored her to the bow.

"Carlos, Carlos," she wailed, struggling to free herself.

"Hold on to her, Rob," boomed Steve.

"You got a lantern?" asked Marty.

"Yeah, in the console."

Marty reached in, plucked out a large spotlight and immediately lit up the surface. "Where the hell are they?" he yelled.

Steve pointed to the port side. "Follow the tide, Marty."

The Southold police pulled up alongside. "What's up?" hollered Officer Wiz.

"Man overboard," yelled Steve.

"Shit," said an annoyed Wiz.

"Actually two! A kid and Timbo."

"In the Gut? Are you kidding me?"

"Over there," yelled Marty, his light bouncing off the water about thirty yards away.

Officer Wiz turned on his searchlight, used it to skim the surface of the water.

Rob pointed, "There they are!"

They saw two heads bobbing in the choppy current.

"You got a Jim-Buoy?" shouted Wiz.

"No. Just this floatation device that came with the boat." Steve held up a fourteen-inch square seat cushion.

"That won't work." From his unit, Officer Wiz threw a thirty-inch round life-ring onto the deck of Steve's boat. "Here, use this."

Steve picked up the ring, put it under his arm and looked at Wiz. "Okay, let's go. We'll follow you."

"No, you go," said Officer Wiz. "This boat is too big to maneuver in the slop. I'll stay behind and keep my searchlight on the swimmers."

"Marty," shouted Steve. "Here, take this buoy and throw it to Timbo when I get close."

Just as Steve got near enough for Marty to toss the life ring, a huge wave rose up and pushed the boat away. Timbo and Carlos went under for a moment but resurfaced quickly.

Steve tried to get the boat closer but was afraid of crashing into the rocks.

"Shit," yelled Marty. "I can't throw this thing that far. My shoulder is fucking shot."

"Rob!" Steve barked. "Take the wheel."

In a flash, Steve grabbed the Jim-Buoy out of Marty's arms and ran to the front of the boat.

"This is a life I can save," he said out loud. With his right hand, he flung the lifesaver though the air and tossed a perfect strike over his good friend's head.

He turned with a satisfied smile, "Swish."

****

I opened my eyes and spied the buoy floating within my reach. "Hold on, Carlos." I seized the round object and held on tight. "Hold on, buddy," I said again, watching as Rob pulled us closer to the stern of the boat.

Steve shut off the engine, grabbed Carlos from me, and put him on the deck. The boy rushed into his mother's arms. "Mama!"

I took hold of the ladder and pulled myself on board.

Rob wrapped me in a bear hug. "Welcome back, Timbo."

I smiled wearily. "Good job, Timbo," said Marty.

"Un-be-fucking-lieve-able," hollered Steve.

The police boat pulled up alongside us again. Loud crackling sounds sputtered from their radio. Wiz shut it off. "I need that buoy back."

Rob tossed it on to him.

Wiz stored it under the seat. "Who is that?" he asked, pointing to Maria.

Silence.

Steve turned away.

"That's my niece," I volunteered.

Wiz stared at me.

"And her son, Carlos."

He glared at me and then shrugged. "Okay. If everyone's safe, I'll be on my way."

Maria smiled.

"Thanks, Joe," I called out.

"Glad I could be of service."

As the police boat left the scene, Carlos let go of his mother's hand and strolled up to Steve. "*Muchas gracias.*"

Steve pulled him close and squeezed him hard. "I'm so glad you're okay."

A happy boy walked back to his mother and sat down next to her. We passed the edge of the lighthouse and slipped into to the gas dock of the marina. Our passengers disembarked quickly as Maria gave me a hug and whispered "*Gracias.*"

I ruffled Carlos' hair. He turned, gave me a smile, and the two strangers, now friends, vanished into the night.

Chapter Forty-Eight

We were still docked at the marina. Rob, Marty, and I stood on the bow of the boat watching two figures made their way through the darkness to the back seat of an old sedan. I smiled, knowing Carlos and Maria were safe.

I turned and noticed an exhausted Steve sitting behind the wheel with his head down. He was crying, and I wondered if his tears were ones of joy, relief or dread. I kept my distance, respecting his privacy, but he called me over. "If only saving Ginny could be that easy," he whispered.

He stood, wiped his eyes with his sleeve. I grabbed him in a bear hug. "I'm so sorry, Bro," I said. "I can't even imagine what you're going through."

Marty walked over, curious. "What's up?"

Steve broke down. "It's Ginny. Ovarian cancer. Stage four."

Marty opened his mouth, but nothing came out. Finally, he spouted, "Oh shit. I'm so sorry. I had no clue."

"I know."

"What can we do?" Marty questioned.

"There's nothing anyone can do."

Unaware of what was going on, Rob came over and slapped Steve on the back. "You were a real hero just now, my friend. Thank God, you majored in Frisbee. It really paid off."

Steve couldn't help but chuckle. "I guess it did."

Marty put his arms around him. "I'm sorry I've been such an asshole."

A moment later Rob's long arms were wrapped around both of them.

"Now, this is getting weird," I cracked. And then went over to join them.

****

We headed back to the sea and set our GPS for home. The clouds had left and the moon was a gift that allowed us to enjoy the view of Orient Beach.

"Wow, what a night this turned out to be," I said. "Look at all these stars."

"The gods are smiling down on us for rescuing Carlos and his mom," said Rob.

"I think we did the right thing," agreed Steve.

"We did the only thing possible," sighed Marty. "I couldn't live with myself, if we hadn't helped."

The door to the head opened and I saw Rob messing with the top of the plastic garbage bag. "What are you doing?" I asked.

"Checking out the merchandise that we risked our lives for." He untied the rope, loosened the sides, and there, on the bathroom floor, stood three green plants, each about two feet tall. "Now, these are a thing of beauty."

"I wouldn't call them beautiful," I said, "but they sure look healthy."

"I thought we were taking only two plants," said Steve.

"I figured that if something went wrong, it would

be wise to have a spare. It's always good to have insurance," I said and winked.

"I'll deliver the plants to my gardener friend," Marty said. "If all goes right, I'll have a check for each of us soon."

"What do we do with the extra plant?" asked Rob.

"I know a guy who says he has a place for it in his blueberry patch," I joked.

"My bushes would welcome the company," smiled Rob.

"Maybe give some seeds to Officer Wiz," I said. "He did us a solid."

We continued our quiet ride past Bug Light into the calmer waters of Greenport Bay.

"I could use a beer," said Marty. "Anyone else?"

"Sure," came a collective response.

He reached into the cooler and popped the tops of three cold summer ales and gave one each to Rob and Steve.

"What about me?" I yelped. "What am I? Chopped liver?"

"You're on those antibiotics. You can't drink."

"Everyone knows that beer and wine don't count."

Steve smiled. It was good to see him relax.

I reached in the cooler and fished out a cold one. "To Carlos," I said, and everyone took a long pull.

"Hey, what about Maria?" said Rob, raising his drink.

"Here's to Maria," said Steve, "And here's to us."

Just then a Bob Dylan classic from the sixties wafted through the speakers.

"Good tune," said Marty.

"I heard that this song was voted the number one

rock and roll composition ever written," said Steve.

"That's right," said an excited Rob. "*Rolling Stone Magazine*—certifiably the expert on rock music for the past fifty years—voted it the best. It was on Dylan's *Highway 61 Revisited* album; I owned a copy back in the day."

"So did I," I said, clinking my bottle to his. "So, here's a question for you guys. What was the magazine named after, the band or the song?"

"That," crooned Marty into his beer, "is a complete unknown."

Steve started cracking up, grabbed the net and began strumming. "But how does it feel, Marty, how does it f-e-e-l to be on the way home, our direction known?"

"We're invincible now," Rob smiled. "It's time we make a deal," he croaked, inhaling his invisible joint.

"I could get used to this," I thought to myself. "Laughing, drinking, and making precious memories with my best buds. Remembering all kinds of useless shit, with a little help from my jellyfish friends."

A word about the author...

James Sleckman, a former sales rep, perfected his craft by writing business memos, articles for trade magazines, and travel journals of his life on the road. Always the storyteller, he began putting prose to the page upon retirement.

He lives on the North Fork with his wife Cathy and their golden retriever Shelby. When he's not working on his second novel, or visiting their son Patrick in Pittsburgh, he's fishing, golfing, or having a cocktail with friends.

Thank you for purchasing
this publication of The Wild Rose Press, Inc.

For questions or more information
contact us at
info@thewildrosepress.com.

The Wild Rose Press, Inc.
www.thewildrosepress.com

9 781509 256013